THE COME-FROM-BEHIND HORSE

And Other Stories

by

Howard Giordano

International Standard Book Number 13:
Hardback 978-1-60452-196-2
Softback 978-1-60452-197-9
eBook 978-1-60452-198-6

International Standard Book Number 10:
Hardback 1-60452-196-1
Softback 1-60452-197-X
eBook 1-60452-198-8

Library of Congress Control Number: 2023942452

BluewaterPress LLC
2922 Bella Flore Ter
New Smyrna Beach, Florida 32168

http://www.bluewaterpress.com

THE COME-FROM-BEHIND HORSE

And Other Stories

This is a collection of "one-off" short stories. Their only commonality is that they deal with the human condition. While the milieu of each story varies, they illustrate the complexities of relationships. Each story emphasizes a strong emotional core, and their characters, authentic and relatable, have very real and relevant conflicts.

Other titles by Howard Giordano

Tracking Terror
The Second Target
Crossing Into Darkness.
The Dark Side of the City

Contents

WHEN THE CONVERSATION ENDS

The mood was strange, not one of her usual "I'm busy wrestling with my personal demons" attitudes. I found her steeped in it all day and I, like a shipwrecked victim reaching out for any piece of flotsam drifting by, interpreted it as remorse. After putting the kids to bed, she surprised me when she came downstairs with a rolled joint from the private stash she hid in her linen drawer. Why I sensed a bit of hope when she handed me the joint to light up confused me.

We'd used grass together many times during our marriage, but I was never more in need to be high than tonight, to be numb, to let the ache slip away, to blot out thoughts of tomorrow, to fight off uncertainties of the future.

Taking a deep drag, I kept the smoke in my lungs as long as possible, the way she showed me when we first met ten years ago, when I was still a conservative cherry. Managing toking and talking was always a problem. We passed the joint back and forth in silence. Dried out, the weed burned quickly.

I watched her fumble with the roach clip and the smoldering remains and wondered, as I always did when we came to this part of the ritual, whether the results were worth the fuss, the legal risks of buying weed, and the logistical inconveniences of smoking it.

"You want any more of this?" she asked, offering the stub pinched between the discolored tips of the holder. Her gaze remained fixed on my tired face, waiting for a reply.

I waved her off and leaned back into the soft cushions of the sofa. When I sensed the onset of lightheadedness, I waited for the veil to move across my brain. Those kids of the sixties, who inhaled the stuff all day and never showed signs, always amazed me. My eyes closed, still red from an earlier uncontrollable outburst of tears. I replayed in my mind the moment, two weeks before, when she exploded the bomb.

"Listen, there's no point in dragging this out," she had begun after we were alone.

I confused her meaning, and not for the first time. I realized later, after days of painful talking, miscommunication was a recurring theme throughout our marriage. She called it being on different wavelengths. I admitted that an eleven-year age spread could account for the problem.

"We should divorce," she had announced, giving no signal, no warning, nothing! Several aftershocks followed. "No, there isn't someone else. No, no, you are a good husband, a good father. I simply don't want to be married anymore. That's all. I feel camouflaged. I look in the mirror, and I see no one I like—No, it's not you. It's marriage. I'm sorry." Her voice had been firm, the way she sounded every time she addressed a women's lib issue. Over the past year, she had transformed into a soldier for the women's liberation movement. Her fellow warriors with their unshaven legs and armpits made me a casualty of her war when they pried open her door.

I suggested changes, such as going back to her old job at the insurance agency in town; offered compromises; made promises to turn her around. My arguments failed. Spent, I agreed on a date to move out.

She tapped the holder, and I stared at the weedy remains dropping into the ashtray to die, along with our marriage. "How you feeling?" I said.

"Okay, I guess," she replied. "A little horny, maybe," she added, making no effort to hide her grin.

"I'll miss that, you know," I said, forcing myself to return a smile.

I looked into the face I'd loved for the past ten years. Why, whenever we shared a joint, did our expression of love reach a level of abandon we could never achieve sober—those moments when we experienced our only form of honest communication?

As if reading my mind, she said, "You'll find others, and they won't need grass." She glanced up at the grandfather clock in the foyer and then up at the ceiling. "Kids should be asleep. One for the road? Might help us make it through tonight."

I struggled to my feet, unsteady on my legs, and she led me by the hand to the stairs—to communicate for the last time, to close the chapter. Tomorrow, I would flip the page.

BLINDED BY SUNLIGHT

Florida's constant sunshine always brought Stella much joy. However, she learned the hard way why they referred to the state as the lightning capital of the US. The agent for this menacing reputation almost did her in.

The white flash bleached out all the objects surrounding her, and the accompanying thunder was immediate and great. Stella felt the building shudder. She lost her balance, falling backward off the step stool, crashing onto her shoulder, and twisting her leg under her body, her limb going one way, her torso choosing the opposite direction. She spent the next four months regretting she did not ask the building's handyman to hang her new shower curtain.

"Rigidly independent" was the accusation her son, Alfred, used when she telephoned him in Connecticut from her hospital bed. He sounded like a lawyer handling a negligence suit. Not a surprise, for that is what he was. Now, she dreaded a second lightning strike, the one forcing her to give up her independence. He never said so, but Stella was confident she heard something in Alfred's voice yesterday when he called to say he was flying down today. She fought the urge to agree with what he might say, that she was too old to continue on her own without help.

It was a pea-green day. She had awakened at seven and managed only a full, breathy yawn. The morning sunshine flooding through the window of her room in assisted living was absent from its assigned post. Light sifting through the morning haze fractured when it came into focus through the glass, reminding her of the first time she witnessed the blinking effect of a revolving strobe. Stella's mood was not unlike the weather—bland and shapeless, struggling to find a lasting form.

She rolled onto her side away from the window, and the pent-up anxieties assembled since the accident spilled out like an overturned jar of marbles. I just know he will insist on my moving back to Darien with him and Peggy. He's going to tell me Keith is out of the house, and I can have his room. Keith, my only sunlight in that world, is no longer there. Alfred knows I cannot afford Sherwood Gardens on my own. I'm here because he helps with my expenses. Thank goodness, I invested the proceeds from the Westport house. The dividends from the sale money and Charles' social security are all the income I have. He will not use that as his argument, I'm sure of it. At least, I hope not. Although, he will plead as he always does, "Now mother, wouldn't it be better if you were closer to us in the event, heaven forbid, something serious happens, and you need us to look after you?" Oh, why can't he understand that my independence is important to me, that without it, I would die?

Stella balanced her head on her elbow and hand, taking in the surroundings like a mother watching her firstborn departing for summer camp. She doubted she would miss the familiarity of the room, the limited space that offered safe haven while her compound fractured leg and dislocated shoulder mended over months of rehabilitation. It felt like a lifetime since the accident. At eighty, Stella considered herself fortunate the healing had not taken longer.

Her thoughts landed on the old married couple who, until recently, lived in the apartment next to her. She recalled how quickly the ailing woman passed away after they moved her blind husband to a nursing home. It was cruel, Stella thought, how rapidly the onset of old age took its toll, not only physically but also emotionally. She felt desperate to survive her setback, her ability to manage alone becoming a gnawing question in her mind. It appeared the matter had lodged itself in Alfred's brain as well.

"Come on, Miss Stella, get a move on," the petite Haitian aide admonished as she entered the room.

Assisted living was unforgiving, Stella thought, always on a schedule, always ready when you were not. This will change today once I'm back in my apartment.

Stella adored her small one-bedroom unit in the corner of the building, her two windows providing generous north and east exposures. She looked at the morning Florida sun streaming through her east-facing bedroom window as her treasure, her reward for enduring all those frigid winters in the Nutmeg State. She enjoyed looking up from her afternoon reading to watch the fragile snowy egrets wading at the edge of the lake that flanked her end of the building.

Upon Stella's return from the hospital to Sherwood Gardens, April Dawson, the manager, assured her, "We'll keep your independent living apartment for you while you're on the assisted side until you're ready to move back. There needs to be a rent adjustment, of course, to cover the added services you'll be receiving while recuperating." Stella telephoned Alfred to tell him, and without pause, he agreed to the increase.

They moved only her double bed, a small nightstand, and an antique six-drawer bureau; the rest of the furniture remained in her apartment.

Sherwood Gardens in Naples, Florida, had become her home the year after Charles died when the court-dictated financial support he had provided since their separation disappeared with him. "He left nothing extra," she confessed to Alfred after the funeral. "It appears he donated most of whatever estate he had accumulated to the horses at the Belmont and Aqueduct Racetracks."

The aide switched on the bathroom light and began the usual preparations for Stella's shower. "Well, get your body out of bed, Miss Stella. Today is the day you been waiting for, ain't that right?"

"Franny, I will miss you the way a Marine recruit misses his drill instructor after boot camp," she said, remembering her young grandson's tales of his early military training. "I'll shower with no bullying from you this morning, thank you."

Francoise returned to the room and smiled, her white teeth glistening between her lips like a warm beacon of light. "Okay, boss lady. You gonna need help with your hair?"

"No, Franny. Today is my Independence Day, similar to Bastille Day in France. Don't you Haitians celebrate that event?" Stella tossed back the bedcovers and rolled up into a sitting position, her feet searching the floor for her slippers. "I'll take care of all my own needs this morning, not that I don't appreciate your offer."

Francoise had been Stella's daily caregiver over her long convalescence. She bathed her, dressed her, and brought her meals on a tray during the early days when mobility was impossible. When she was well enough to leave her bed, it was Francoise who pushed her in a wheelchair to the dining room.

Stella didn't require it any longer, but out of habit she reached for the brass-handle cane hooked on the end of her headboard and levered herself upright. Francoise watched her with interest and smiled again when she took several steps with apparent ease.

"Don't bother to make up my bed," Stella called as she disappeared into the bathroom. "I'll do it myself after they move it back over. I can remember how it's done." She paused to give Francoise time to absorb her humor. "And if not, I can always ask Alfred to do it for me when he arrives this afternoon. He enjoys doing things for me. Alfred, the doting son. He always places his mother's needs first, though not her feelings. You know, I can always second-guess Alfred's reaction to matters concerning me—a role reversal of parent and helpless child. He needs my dependency more than I need his. So unnatural. He also has Charles' stubbornness, which is going to be my real problem today. Franny, are you listening?"

Though she couldn't see Francoise's face, Stella could hear her snickering. She had burdened the aide with this litany of complaints before, and each time Francoise would chide her for being pessimistic. "If I were negative like you," Francoise would remind her, "I would have given up after the Tonton Macoute tortured and killed my father and mother. But look, I am here with my son and everything is good again." Stella's four-month dependency on the Haitian woman had developed a bond they both enjoyed, despite almost two generations in age difference. There was much one could admire about Francoise, Stella acknowledged. Her stoicism and fierce independence impressed her the most.

"Franny, are you there?" she called from the bathroom, but she failed to receive a reply. Stella stood rock-like, holding on to the porcelain basin with both hands as if needing it for support. She studied her reflection in the mirror. Worry and tension, absent these last two months, now beginning to return, disturbed her. Her white shock of hair was thick and full. Stella recalled Miriam and Blanche, her two dining companions, and their constant carping about falling hair. She counted herself fortunate. Her tanned skin was taut, and very few lines on her face were visible. She could lop off ten years and pass for seventy. Oh, why doesn't Alfred understand? I'm not feeble, and I don't need his ministering. I don't want to spend the rest of my days under his roof, suffering through Connecticut winters again.

* * *

The plane arrived at the Fort Myers Airport on time, and Alfred's rental car pulled up under the portico entrance of Sherwood Gardens just before noon. He stepped out of the rented Ford, and Stella opened her arms and smiled.

Alfred, attired in a soft, open-collared golf shirt and khaki trousers, wasn't wearing socks with his loafers. He had left his regular lawyer-like appearance in the closet, back in Darien. All good signs.

"Shall we go somewhere for lunch?" he asked after greeting his mother with a tentative embrace and a brush of lips across her cheek. Stella could never be sure whether she or Charles was to blame for Alfred's inability to show affection. Lord knows, he had seen little enough of it at home. She remembered whenever her husband came home, he was inebriated or in a belligerent mood, a hangover from one of his many unhappy workdays at his New York City advertising agency.

"Why not have lunch here in the apartment? It will give us more time to talk," she said, knowing the unspoken meaning of this familial-sounding suggestion was, "Look how I can take care of myself."

"Sure, if that's what you'd prefer, but you haven't had time to settle in yet. I figured it would be easier if we went out."

"No, no, I have everything I need for a nice lunch right here. Franny, bless her heart, shopped for me this morning before she came on duty. How is Peggy? Why didn't she come with you? Go . . . go . . . sit down," she said, directing him to the sofa in the living room.

Alfred chose the Queen Anne wing chair instead. "Peg is back working for the interior decorating firm," he answered. "She had several client meetings this week. Couldn't break away."

Stella prepared lunch in the small kitchenette corner of the apartment. She had selected a new skirt and blouse to wear for the reunion, and Francoise had helped her with her hair this morning despite her earlier protest. Stella, feeling on top of her game, drew a new sense of confidence from her reprised role of nourishing mother.

"Is Keith up at school?" she asked.

Alfred put down the album he was examining, family photos full of sentimental memories going back to Charles and Stella's early married years. There were snapshots of him as a child and pictures of his father in his later Jekyll and Hyde period, even one with Stella and Charles during happier days standing at the rail watching the morning workouts on the Saratoga Racecourse. "Yes, he is," he said, "finishing his senior year. He's considering going to grad school."

"How wonderful! Those four years in the Marine Corps gave him time to change his outlook on life. I'm glad he didn't go to college right out of prep school."

"So am I," Alfred agreed. "It gave him time to grow up and gave me a chance to put enough money away for his tuition."

Typical of Alfred, she thought. Her son's ability to pay for Keith's education was never a question in Stella's mind. Peggy had flaunted his high six-figure income from his firm's partnership on more than one occasion. Alfred, for reasons Stella failed to understand, did not share his wife's concept of his financial well-being. He often approached ordinary expenditures as though he were a child of the depression era.

"Is Keith considering law school, perhaps?" When she said it, she remembered Charles' reaction when Alfred informed him he wanted to pursue a law degree. Charles had always been vocal about his criticism of lawyers. Despite his reluctance, he agreed to pay for Alfred's law school. Stella suspected Alfred's career choice to become a lawyer was his way of putting his father behind him as far as possible.

"Believe it or not, Keith is interested in their business program—marketing. He does a lot of creative writing now in his spare time. It's darn good, at least the stuff he lets me read."

Stella stopped slicing the celery and put the knife down on the cutting board. She turned to face Alfred. "Oh, my!" she said. "Do you suppose he's leaning toward becoming an advertising copywriter, like your father?"

Alfred laughed. "Mother, you make it sound like safecracking."

"No, no, I'm surprised, is all. Keith's undergraduate major is history, isn't it?"

Alfred nodded, and Stella turned back to the cutting board.

What do you know? It seems the creative genes in this family skipped a generation and are now back on track. Her mind flashed to something else. A rush of memories caused her to chill. "I hope his curriculum doesn't include the two-martini lunch."

"You don't have to worry about that. Keith has a clear head about his future, and he rarely drinks. Oh, maybe a beer now and then. Speaking of the future, will it be okay to make the trip up north for his graduation in June? What's the doctor say about traveling?"

Stella froze. June? This was February, four months away. Unable to control her surprise, she turned back to Alfred. "Didn't you . . . didn't you come down here to talk me into moving back to Darien with you and Peggy . . . I mean, because you're worried about me being on my own?"

Alfred snickered. "Are you kidding? Where did that idea come from? I came down for a couple of days to help you get resettled and to see what I could do for you. Move you back with us? Woman, are you trying to break up my marriage? Besides, you've been on your own forever. You would find living with us a crushing bore and a hindrance to your swinging, single lifestyle. Seriously, mother, aren't you happy here?" Alfred rose from the chair and approached Stella with a look of concern. "Because we can always find another—"

Stella rushed to him, wrapping him in her arms before he could finish. "Oh, yes, I'm very happy here." She held on, pressing her head to his chest forever until he pulled back. She looked up at her son with a mother's love, seeing him with fresh eyes for the first time in ages. "Don't pay me any mind, Alfred. Something must have rattled my head when I took that fall. I'm going to be fine here. I know it now."

Alfred returned to the wing chair and sat down. "Mother, you've cared for yourself all your life. Why should you stop now?"

"Alright," she declared, "now that we've settled that, let's have lunch. You starved?"

* * *

"Franny, Franny, come over here before you leave," Stella shouted into the phone. "Alfred left for his hotel, and I want to tell you something. You won't believe it. You simply won't believe it."

Francoise giggled into the mouthpiece. "I think already I know what you're going to say. I'm not surprised, boss lady, by anything you would tell me."

"Oh, Franny, don't be smug. Come over here when you can." Stella hung up, went to the window to enjoy the afternoon sunlight, and smiled when she caught sight of two snowy egrets zigzagging toward the water.

HUGGABLE TOM

Raised on a small farm, Paco Velasquez took early rising for granted. "Getting up at four-thirty every morning," he would say, "is the price for doing something I love and get paid too." Those outside his world considered him crazy. Some inside thought that, but for a different reason.

The hour had the morning pitched in blackness. A mud-mired horse path circling the barn was the only sign of the recent downpour that had soaked the Belmont Park Racetrack. Although the wind had died down, the air was sticky and reminiscent of August at the upstate Saratoga track.

Paco crossed the muddy path between the paved roadway and the barn filled with Thoroughbreds. Each step sent him sinking into the sludge, producing a suction that clung to his worn, scruffy riding boots. Low-wattage bulbs on the shedrow's wooden ceiling splashed their illumination at intervals on the sandy floor along the long row of stalls. The pool of light collecting midway down the shedrow opposite

Huggable Tom's stall was a homing beacon for Paco. His steps crunched as he made his way across the grainy surface, past the series of half doors and quiet stirrings from within.

He reined up at Tom's stall and heard the four-year-old roan colt mutter, *Jeez, that time already? Seems like I just got to sleep.*

"Morning, you old plug," Paco said as he swung open the half door to enter the straw-strewn cubicle. He grabbed the feed tub and water bucket and hauled them outside. The horse had emptied both containers.

"Thirsty last night, huh?" he said and tied the Thoroughbred to the wall while fighting off his nudging head.

Aw, is that necessary? I ain't goin' nowhere.

"Hold still, Tom, you know the routine." He reached for the bucket. "Sorry. Can't do nothin' to change it. Stay cool, man. Be right back with a refill. Okay?"

"*Hola, que tal?*" The voice came from the semi-darkened end of the barn.

"Lopez, *amigo. Como esta?*" Paco moved toward the voice and the spigot, and reaching the water source, he opened the valve and filled the bucket.

"Hey, Paco, missed you last night at Esposito's. *Qué pasó?*"

Enrique Lopez, a groom from Mexico with over ten years of experience on the backstretch, was at the opening of the end stall, removing the standing bandages from the legs of a chestnut filly. His head of curly black hair and an angular, pockmarked face sat atop a lean, sinewy body that came with a decade of hard, sweaty work on a racetrack. Lopez was a pro. Most of the others in the barn considered him one bad dude. You called him either Enrique or Lopez and never Henry. The scars from knife slashes decorating his arms like Olympic medals signaled to everyone in barn number 26 not to take the Mexican lightly. Paco's trainer had warned him a few times to keep his distance.

"Ah, man, I was too tired for any more boozing. My head still hurts from the other night." Paco dropped his voice to a whisper and added, "Gotta move. Tom's in the fifth today, a six-furlong claimer."

"Wadda ya whispering for, man? 'Fraid the horse'll hear?"

"Yeah, right. He always gets sweaty . . . you know, and uptight on a race day."

"Hey, Paco, you *loco*! You talk like the colt understands everything and talks back to you. Weird, man. Everybody thinks you lost it. Know what I mean?"

"Damn, Lopez! Horses do understand. You been on the backstretch long enough to see that. They're not *estupido* like everyone says."

"Yeah, but they don't talk. *Comprende?*"

Paco picked up the filled water bucket and started back toward Tom's stall. He was sure more conversation with Lopez would only escalate into an explosion of tempers.

Five years ago, Paco arrived from Panama at seventeen and sought employment on the backstretch of Belmont Park. The trainer, Johnny Camposino, hired him for his small public stable. His initial chores were the usual stuff: mucking out stalls and walking hots. In no time, he moved up to groom, impressing Johnny with his reliability and talent for controlling the huge beasts in his charge. From the outset, it was clear the roly-poly trainer had developed a father-like attitude toward the young Panamanian.

Paco went to work removing the horse's standing bandages. Each time he reached the end of a roll freeing the fetlock, Tom expelled a noise that sounded like aah.

Within the next quarter hour, the barn buzzed with hot walkers, grooms, and assistant trainers. Paco's tasks during this early period never varied. He attended to the needs of the horse and the three other Thoroughbreds in his charge.

After brushing down each one, he would sponge the animals, taking care not to expose them to an early morning chill. Sunlight showed through the dirty barn windows as the track veterinarian arrived for his scheduled examinations. The medical man looked over several mares at the front of the barn before moving down the line.

"How you this morning, Paco?" the vet inquired upon reaching Huggable Tom's stall.

"The horse ready for his checkup?"

"*Si*, Doc. He's in great shape. But, *por favor*, don't say nothin' about him racing today. Okay? No reason to upset him too soon. You know what I mean?"

"Paco, you actually believe your colt understands words, don't you?"

"Hey, Doc, he does. *Absolutamente!* I see it all the time."

"Okay, Paco, I won't breathe a word. Bring him out and let's have a look-see."

The vet completed his examination with routine professionalism and pronounced the horse sound for his race. He delayed until the groom returned Tom to his stall before whispering. "Okay, he's good to go." A smile danced across the vet's face.

"*Oye*, Paco. Want to grab some breakfast after Eddie takes the colt?" The invitation came from Lopez as he worked the tack on his chestnut filly, readying her for a morning workout on the training track.

"Okay, *amigo*, but I'm waitin' for Eddie. He ain't here yet."

A few moments later, the exercise rider appeared at the front of the shedrow. He had stopped to talk with an assistant trainer.

"Hey, Eddie, c'mon, man," Paco called to him. "Tom's waiting for you, tacked and ready to go." The rider approached, and Paco met him halfway. "Remember, man," he said quietly, "a slow jog today." Then, in a whisper, he said, "He's in the fifth."

"What are you, the trainer now? Where's Johnny?"

"He's at the gap on the training track, by the clocker's stand. Said he'll meet you and Tom there." Paco's tone could not disguise his feeling of envy.

When Paco first showed up on the racetrack's backstretch, he was a short, bowlegged teenager. While his bowlegged condition remained, during the next five years, the young groom grew six inches and gained twenty pounds, forever destroying his hopes of making it as a jockey.

* * *

Cathy's Backstretch Kitchen reverberated with shouts and loud, hurried conversations in both English and Spanish. Grooms and hot walkers occupied the linoleum-covered tabletops, gulping black coffee and munching buttered rolls amidst the odor of fried eggs and sausages.

The Mexican sat across from Paco at a table in one corner of the eatery. He had Paco's Daily Racing Form spread out while he studied the past performance chart of the fifth race.

"*Amigo*," Lopez said, without looking up, "the morning line has your horse at twelve to one. He's better than that, no?"

"Don't know, man. He had a few nice workouts this week. I mean, he gets so uptight sometimes. If only his jock could relax him better. He likes to run but—"

"How you know that, Paco? He tell you?" Lopez chuckled.

Paco's pulse quickened. "Yeah, man, he did."

"Well, he tell you he gonna win?"

"He don't even know he's gonna race yet." He said it before he realized Lopez was playing with him.

Lopez continued to tease. "Well, man, when you gonna tell him?"

Paco took another swallow of coffee and stood. "You think a horse doesn't know when he's gonna race? The minute the muzzle goes on, he knows. First change in routine, his ears go up. Lopez, sometimes you so dense, you—"

"*Cuidado, chico.* You gettin' nasty. Don't appreciate that."

Paco reached across the table, gathered in The Daily Racing Form, folded it into a semi-roll, and tucked it into his back pocket. "Gotta go."

"Wait," Lopez said, getting to his feet and following him toward the kitchen exit. "I ain't making fun of you, man. Honest."

"You coulda fooled me," Paco said without breaking stride.

"No, man. I only find it hard to believe, that's all. But if you say the horse talks to you, I'm okay with that. I'm your *amigo*, right? What I mean is . . ." Lopez scanned the kitchen . . . "you should be more secret in front of the other guys. You know what I'm saying, man?"

Paco didn't answer. The two grooms walked together in silence along the paved road toward their barn. When they arrived, Lopez stopped at the opening of the shedrow, and taking hold of Paco's arm, he said, "*Momentito*, Paco. I wanna ask you something."

Paco yanked free. He stared into the dark, menacing eyes of Lopez and said, "What? Make it quick."

"Look, maybe you can ask the horse how he's gonna do today? After he finds out he's running, I mean."

"C'mon, Lopez. Lay off."

"No, no, *amigo*, I mean it. I wanna know."

"What for?"

"Well, if he feels he's got a shot, maybe we can get down a few bucks on him. You know what I mean? Hey, man, why waste a little inside dope? Right?"

Paco spotted Johnny coming toward them from the training track. Huggable Tom was right behind with Eddie aboard. He worried the trainer had seen him talking with Lopez.

"The horse is here," Paco said. "See you later," and quick-stepped away.

Lopez followed. "Wadda ya say, man? Will you ask him or not?"

Paco slowed and looked back. "What?"

"The horse . . . the race. Ask him, *amigo*. Okay?"

"I'll think about it," Paco said, and retreated into Tom's stall to await the return of the horse.

Paco took the Thoroughbred's reins after Eddie dismounted. With dispatch, the groom removed the horse's tack. He led Tom outside into the warm sunshine, where a hot walker waited on the small patch of grass that somehow survived the trod of hooves. Paco turned the rein over to the youngster while he coupled the brass connector of a hose to the spigot on the barn wall. A half-twist of the knob and Paco dribbled a soft stream over the length of the colt.

Tom stood still, enjoying the second bath of the morning, flinching whenever the flow washed over a sensitive area. Even when Paco placed the nozzle between the horse's ears, allowing a gentle river to cascade down his head and face, the colt seemed to luxuriate in his groom's attention.

When he disconnected the hose, Paco tossed a plain mesh blanket over Tom's back. He released the animal to his hot walker for a twenty-minute circuit around the barn to cool him down. The path, muddy from the early morning rain, had splashed against Tom's legs. When the hot-walker returned with Tom, Paco brushed down the animal and cleaned his hooves.

Once back in the stall, Paco re-wrapped the colt's fetlocks. *Not too tight, eh*, Huggable Tom whined.

"You know, if you didn't kick yourself all the time, we might not need them."

Ah, I don't do it any more than these other nags.

Paco completed the bandaging. "Hold still a moment while I slip this on."

Wadda ya doin'?

The quick, jerking motion of the horse's head made it difficult for Paco to secure the muzzle in place. "Damn it! Stay still."

What's goin' on? I gotta race today? Why didn't you tell me?

"Figured you'd find out soon enough. Stop pulling away, will you? And quit worrying."

Wadda ya mean, quit worryin'? My last time out, I made a fool of myself, didn't I?

"This one's six furlongs. Last time Johnny was trying you out at a mile. Too long for you."

Yeah, tell me about it. I needed a taxi at the top of the stretch to make it home. Thought my lungs would bust.

"This distance is well within your range, and besides, you're up against nothing special. You faced most of them before."

Like who? Let me have a look at The Form.

Paco unrolled the newspaper and turned to the page with the fifth-race chart.

Huggable Tom snorted as he tried to nibble at his hay bale. *Hell, with this muzzle on, I can't even get near it.*

"That's the idea. Okay, here's who you're up against," Paco said, looking down the list of entries. "Band-Aid. Fourteen-to-one."

Finished ahead of him three weeks ago, didn't I?

"Right. Next, Mogambo's Child. He's six-to-one. You were fourth to him back in May at six furlongs."

Oh, yeah. I remember. His jock claimed foul on the winner for interference during the stretch run. It didn't stand up.

"Next, Twelfth Night. He's the favorite. Four-to-one. Got beat by him in your maiden race last year. Five and a half furlongs. He won by a length."

I was close. Haven't seen him since. How's he done?

"Hasn't won another. What's that tell you?"

Lucky the first time. Okay, who's next?

While Paco reviewed the eight competitors one by one, the colt broke into a sweat, gobs of white, frothy moisture collecting on his neck and running down to his shoulders.

Paco glanced up from *The Racing Form*. "Look at you. You're all wet. Why do you get so worked up?"

I don't know. Hyper, I guess.

"Morning line has you twelve-to-one."

Pfft! I deserve better odds than that. Okay, I don't win in my last six starts. Been in the money a couple of times, ain't I?

"Well, what about today's race? You got a shot?"

A bunch of crows! Of course, I do—I think.

"Well, do you or don't you?"

Jeez, don't get pushy. Let's see. Most of the time I'm the early speed, right? If my jock holds me back a little longer going down the backside until we hit the turn at the top of the stretch, I bet I have enough left to?

"Bet? Did you say bet?"

Nah, you know what I mean.

"Oh, for a moment I thought you were gonna say you were a mortal lock, and I should get down a bet on you."

Wadda ya talkin'? You don't bet, do you?

"Usually I don't."

Hey, so don't start now, or you'll give me something to really sweat over.

"Well, you gonna win or not? Don't matter much to me. To tell the truth, it's Lopez wants to know. He's gonna bet you."

Yeah, no kidding? His interest ain't exactly flattering. Let's say I got a shot. Leave it at that. Okay?"

"All right, sport. Time for some rest." Paco picked up the excess rolls of bandage, moved out of the stall, and closed the door behind him. "I'll be back in two hours with a half ration of oats."

Big deal!

"That's all you ever get on a race day."

* * *

At a certain time of the day, part of the Belmont grandstand overhang often eclipsed the late afternoon fiery yellow ball, leaving the rest of the track bathed with sunshine. This day was no different. The roofline, traveling the entire length of the homestretch, cast a broad shadow across the running surface, originating opposite the eighth pole and carrying beyond the finish line.

Paco and Lopez had positioned themselves within the darkened area at the railing gap through which outriders led the equine contestants out onto the track for the post-parade. The two grooms had the perfect spot to watch the stretch run of the race. However, their ground-level position limited their viewing angle and prevented them from seeing across the vast, grassy infield of the racing oval. The gate crew loaded the horses into the starting gate on the other side, and the large, green tote board on the front edge of the infield loomed up, also obstructing their view.

"Your horse looked sweaty in the barn," Lopez said, waiting for the track announcer to begin his call of the race. "He okay?"

"Yeah, sure," Paco answered. "He settled down on the walk over to the paddock."

"Hope so, man. Got down big, you know. Fifty bucks to win since the colt got the inside post position. He's only six-to-one now. They must be bettin' him a little. You get down?"

"Nah. Didn't have time after I got Tom to the paddock."

"Want a piece of my action?" Lopez asked.

"No, thanks, that's okay. Bothers me to bet on my own horses."

The groom glared at him. "He gonna win, right? He told you he would, no?"

"Well, yeah. He said he had a shot. Told you that, didn't I?"

"One more to load," the track announcer's voice informed them over the public address system.

Lopez gave Paco a high five. "Okay, man, here we go."

There was a long pause before they heard the race caller groan, "Aaannnd they're off!"

"He get out of the gate okay?" Lopez asked, eyeing the tote board and waiting for the initial posting of numbers to show the early running order of the first four horses.

"Yeah, yeah, there he is," Paco cried out. "One . . . six . . . three . . . eight. Went to the lead like I knew."

"Good," said Lopez. "Hope he stays there."

By the time the field cleared the tote board sightlines, the horses were in full gallop halfway down the backstretch. The two grooms strained to hear the track announcer's call of the race.

"Down the backstretch, heading toward the first turn," the caller recited, "it's Huggable Tom in front, Twelfth Night a close second, Mogambo's Child back a length in third, and Hagley fourth by a half." The caller's drone continued. "Four lengths back to Campfire. Star Pilot, followed by Dance Ace, Sweet Revenge, with Band-Aid the trailer. The time for the first quarter, twenty-three and three."

The pace was not particularly fast, Paco thought, and in Tom's favor. He figured his jock had the horse relaxed.

The nine Thoroughbreds, lungs bursting for air and under the occasional urging by the whip of their riders, approached the long curve of the racing oval. Lopez stared at the tote board. The horses hit the turn, and they posted a new sequence.

"One . . . three . . . six . . . eight," cried Lopez. "We still up there."

Paco could follow the Thoroughbreds where the field lengthened out and they reached the flatter section of the curve. He listened to the announcer's call of the entries again, the last time he would hear it clearly.

Behind him, from the clubhouse and grandstand seats, and along the rail at trackside, Paco heard crowd murmurs, low at first and growing louder in sync with each stage of the race. After the horses navigated the last section of the curve, they came into the final turn of the racing oval. The buzz surrounding Paco swelled louder, and before long, the announcer's call gradually faded, submerged beneath the crowd noise.

Sixteen thousand heads strained toward the top of the stretch, eyes fixed on the rainbow of colorful jockey silks glistening over the massive Thoroughbreds. The horses moved into the straightaway to face the grueling challenge of the long stretch run.

Belmont Park came alive with booming voices urging their selections to the finish line. A tingling sensation electrified Paco as if they had wired his body into the amplifier that modulated the rising sound level. No matter how many times he watched a race, any race, the crowd reaction always produced this phenomenon. The noise increased, and so did the tingling until both hit their absolute maximum levels. This never varied; always when the horses came into unobstructed view precisely one thousand and ninety-seven feet away.

A head-on perspective made the field appear spread across the sun-drenched track. The lead horse dove hard to keep the inside rail position. The tote board posted the time for the half: forty-six seconds flat.

"Damn, faster than I thought," shouted Paco. "Hope he got something left."

For a third time, the running numbers changed, and Lopez screamed his reaction. "One . . . six . . . seven . . . three. Goddamn, he gonna go wiretowire. C'mon you son-of-a-bitch, stay up there."

Now Paco could spot the yellow, red, and white colors of Tom's silks in front. His heart pumped. He banged the heels of his hands against the track railing, keeping tempo with each stride of the horse.

"Go . . . go . . . go . . . go . . . go." The crescendo of screaming horseplayers assaulted his ears. The tingling sensation was almost painful.

Nearing the eighth pole, Huggable Tom and his nemesis, Twelfth Night, were in lockstep, flying down the soft, track surface with hooves that never seemed to touch down. The rest of the field trailed them. The contest was between the two leaders.

Huggable Tom, a full head in front, raced as he always did: his tongue dangling out one side of his mouth—his long tail swishing with each stride—his muscles and veins standing out on his extended body—the shiny sweat coating him from head to tail—the moisture accenting his form as though he were a marble sculpture under a spotlight.

It happened so fast, Paco might have missed it. At the point across the track where bright sunlight ended, and the long dark shadow began, Huggable Tom leaped, trying to avoid a perceived danger that wasn't there. It was over in a blink of an eye. Only the switched position of the combatants was proof it happened at all. That and the fact Twelfth Night hit the wire first.

At once, the din went silent, as if some mythical symphony conductor had slashed the air with his baton to signal the conclusion of the concert. At the same time, Paco's tingling also died.

* * *

Paco knocked on the screen door. Dried paint flaked under his knuckles.

"Get the hell in here, kid!"

Johnny had never called him that. Paco thought he sounded miffed.

Pulling open the door, the groom stepped into the official headquarters of J.C. Stables, a twelve-by-twelve windowless room at the far end of barn 26. A metal desk from the forties, a slat-back swivel chair, abused for many years by Johnny's wide frame, two wobbly side chairs in need of glue, and a small cot pushed against one wall were the total furnishings.

Johnny pointed to one chair. "Sit down, Paco."

No question, he was pissed. The groom obeyed and sat quietly while the trainer continued talking on the phone.

Paco gazed around the room, taking in the Spartan appointments. His focus settled on the ornate wooden coat stand behind Johnny's desk. It accommodated mostly tack. A saddlecloth, cap and goggles, shadow roll, and several pairs of blinkers dangled freely from its curving arms, forming the effect of a still-life sculpture.

Thumbtacked to the wall opposite were pictures of famous Thoroughbred stakes winners, torn from the pages of the Richard Stone Reeves book, *Decade of Champions*. Johnny had given Paco his copy of this collection of equine portraits for Christmas last year.

The trainer hung up the phone and turned toward the groom. His voice boomed across the desk. "Paco, what the hell's going on?" Paco flashed to the stories he'd heard about Johnny's youth, growing up on the streets of East New York, and New Jersey, kicking ass. He considered bolting for the door.

"Wadda ya mean, John? About the race today?"

"No, goddamn it, not the race—yeah, it's about the race too, but right now I'm talking about you and Lopez."

Paco pretended not to understand and stared at him.

"How many times I tell you, stay away from Lopez outside the barn?"

He remembered this morning when Johnny spotted him with the Mexican groom. "Man, we were only shootin' the breeze."

"Shootin' the breeze, my ass. You tell Lopez the horse gonna win, and you hear it from Tom himself? Came in here after the race screaming you were a certifiable nut case. That you hear the horse talking to you, and it cost him fifty bucks."

Paco was perspiring. The sweat trickled from his armpit area and down the inside of both arms. The tee shirt he wore provided no help at all.

"I didn't tell him—"

"Don't lie to me, Paco. I hear the rumblings around here—about you having conversations with the horse."

Paco looked again toward the door.

"Listen to me, damn it. I don't want you going around telling anybody Tom talks to you. You understand? 'Specially that loony, Lopez. You ever see him explode after a few shots of rum in his snoot? At Esposito's? He's crazy. You messin' with the wrong guy. I'm warning you."

".John, I handicapped the race myself. Honest. I only said the horse had a shot. That's all."

"Cut the shit. I know what's going on." The trainer had lowered his voice. "Happened once when I was a kid, breaking my hump for that public riding academy in Central Park."

"Wadda ya mean?" Paco asked.

"What I mean is, the only voice you hear is the one you invent in your head. Right?"

Paco sat up in the chair.

"I mean, you got so tight with the horse you imagine him speaking to you. Right? Am I right?" A knowing grin formed on the trainer's face.

"Yeah, I guess," Paco said.

"Damn straight, I am. Hey, Paco, don't make me have to break up your love affair by taking Tom from you. I don't want to do that. You understand? No more goddamn conversations. Okay?"

"Okay. No more."

"And Lopez. Stay the hell away. Please? He's nothing but trouble."

"Sure, and I'll keep Tom away, too. The horse ain't crazy about him, either."

Johnny sat motionless, staring at the gallery of Thoroughbred champions tacked to his wall. Paco got to his feet, and the trainer turned back. "He run a goddamn good race today, didn't he?"

"Yeah, his best one yet."

Johnny shook his head. "Damn! I can't understand the horse jumpin' a shadow that way. He never got spooked before, even as a two-year-old. Shadows never bothered him. Beats the shit out of me. Got any ideas?"

"Well, I got one," Paco said, heading toward the door.

"What's that? Because I need something to tell his connections."

"Like I said before, Huggable Tom ain't crazy about Lopez."

"Get the hell outta here!" Johnny yelled.

* * *

The next morning Paco arrived at the barn and found the Mexican sitting outside Tom's stall astride an overturned water bucket. The groom was facing the colt's protruding head, studying his drowsy eyes, when Paco approached.

"Oye, Lopez, que pasa?"

"Nothin', man, just waiting for you. Wanted to ask the horse . . . ah, I mean, I wanted to ask you something."

Paco became cautious. "What?"

Lopez got to his feet. "I heard Johnny say yesterday he gonna run the colt in the Sword Dancer in a couple of weeks."

"Yeah, what about it?"

"So if you hear any dope on the race, you let me know straight away. Right, *amigo?*"

"I don't know, man. Johnny, he don't want me talking about Tom's races with anybody anymore." He watched Lopez's expression as he continued. "But, if I hear anything . . ." Paco grinned as he let his voice trail off.

"Great, man. So later at Cathy's for breakfast. Okay?" Lopez didn't wait for an answer. He strode toward the rear of the barn and disappeared into the bulb-cast shadows of the shedrow.

"Maybe," Paco mumbled, "if I have time." The smugness in his tone made him smile again. When he looked over at Tom, the colt's head was bobbing up and down at a furious pace.

FAIR PLAY

The windy avenue was awash with short skirts raining shapely legs, and all I could think about was food. I must have been out of my mind or very hungry, I pushed my way to the counter of the Lantern coffee shop to grab a fast bite. Fifteen minutes later, she entered the restaurant. Only the squishing noise of the padded stool indicated someone had slipped in next to me. I felt her proximity and sensed her vibrations. A quick turn of my head and I glimpsed her dark, quizzical eyes darting with lightning speed. They flew first to my face, past my slumped-over shoulders, down the line of hunched forms at the crowded counter, and finally, like a homing pigeon, they fluttered back to a soft landing on my face, where they remained.

I was conscious of her stare. My head-bob in her direction showed she was smiling. Her display of white, scrubbed pearls flashing behind the ruby paint of her full mouth was dazzling. She leaned in close to my ear and her warm breath landed on my cheek. The din of clanging plates and short-order shouts muted her soft, cultured voice.

"Excuse me, what's that you've ordered?"

My eyes lowered, and I examined the toasted sandwich as though seeing it for the first time. Its crisp edges exuded yellow, melted American cheese, and wedges of red tomatoes. I turned back to the woman. Her smile remained. "A grilled cheese and tomato." I took a second furtive peek. "Yeah, I know. It tastes better than it looks."

She reminded me of Melina Kanakaredes, the Greek-American TV actor from CSI: NY, who played Detective Stella Bonasera; the same long, curly hair that cascaded beyond her shoulders and framed her chiseled cheekbones and a strong, jutting jaw. An aquiline nose hinted at her ethnic origin, and while she researched my sandwich, I imagined her in a skimpy costume undulating to exotic Greek music. She sat with her back straight at a perfect ninety-degree angle to the counter, looking haughty but sexy.

Her critical scrutiny continued until a pair of black pants and a white shirt interrupted. Order pad at the ready, the counterman's fingers rested on the menu inserted between the napkin holder and the ketchup bottle. "You wanna see the menu or you know what you want?"

Her reply was unhesitating. "That's all right. I want a tuna salad sandwich on whole-wheat toast with lettuce, dry, no mayonnaise, and tea with lemon, please. Oh, and may I have a glass of water?" She turned back to me. "Sorry," she said, as though she had insulted my judgment.

"No problem. I usually have the tuna salad on Tuesdays, only on rye toast." I wondered how old she was and if she was married. She wore no ring.

Again, a smile lighted her face. "Oh, you come here a lot? Must be a good place." Her words spilled out, and I inhaled them as I would the bouquet of expensive wine.

"No, but it's convenient," I said. She searched my face, waiting for me to continue. "I work nearby. . . up the street . . . across Sixth . . . Sixteen forty-five . . . the Burlington Building." When my tongue began forming the ad agency's floor number, I swallowed.

Her silky voice enveloped me again. "Oh, my. What a coincidence. We—my law firm, that is—recently moved there. This is our first week in the building, and I'm now exploring the neighborhood for places to have lunch."

The white shirt and black pants delivering the tuna sandwich cut off any opportunity to keep the dialogue going. We ate in silence surrounded by greasy smells, shouts of coded lunch orders, and the sounds of sizzling burger patties the cook tossed about on his hotplate. I finished my grilled cheese and reached across for the inserted menu. I rarely had dessert, but I read down the list anyway, hoping to stall until I could come up with a way to jump-start the conversation.

Before I could, a hand slapped down the check, picked up my empty plate, and preempted my options. The culprit asked in the practiced, impatient voice of restaurant countermen, "Something else, or that gonna be it?"

"No, no, nothing else." I reinserted the menu between the ketchup and the napkins.

She nodded as I stood, and she studied me while I sifted through the change in my pocket, but instead, I laid a dollar bill on the counter for the tip and turned toward the door.

"Bye," she said, "I guess I'll see you again."

She spoke the statement in a manner that would pass for simple civility anywhere. Except, this was New York City, where one uttered pleasantries only with guarded encouragement.

"I certainly hope so," I answered.

* * *

Waiting in the small plaza in front of my glass and steel office building, I shifted my weight from one foot to the other like a child requiring a bathroom. I took a position downwind of the plaza's circulating fountain, trying, with little success, to avoid the spray. The March winds kept changing direction and sabotaging my effort. I hoped she would show up soon before I got drenched. My trouser legs whipped in the wind like a ship's pennants on a stormy sea. Despite temperatures in the low thirties, I was perspiring.

I sensed old John Henry was cooling down as I waited in the plaza. Not since high school, when they tagged me with the locker room nickname of Randy Andy, had I experienced the old penchant for boners in public. I smiled at the sudden rush of memories.

As a teenager, I indulged in a lot of sexual fantasies, although I never considered myself a horny kid. My inventions were ordinary, the kind most fifteen-year-old kids picture goes on behind the walls of Hugh Hefner's Playboy Mansion.

These whimsical imaginings would materialize with disturbing frequency on the City-Transit bus I rode home from school. My imagination would leap alive, ignited by some middle-aged woman seated across the aisle who, in my juvenile point of view, possessed an erotic magnetism. An abstract quality, I admit, and one I could never define to the satisfaction of my teammates on the football team of Plainview High School. Hell, being sexy didn't require a pretty face and a shapely body. Even as a teenager, I recognized eroticism transcended physical beauty. Try explaining that concept to a bunch of buck-naked, mud-soaked, cut-and-bruised juvenile Neanderthals in a locker room shower.

During my rides home, my focus would remain fixed on my target. I would visualize her undressed or, if I dared, fancied her taking part with me in a particular sexual act. I realize now, given my youth, my inhibitions stood in the way of fulfilling my whimsies.

Steeped in these heated images, I would become aware I had awakened old John Henry. Often awkward, I found myself too embarrassed to stand when the bus chugged to my stop at the street corner. Red-faced, I would remain seated long enough to permit my erection to cool down, and then backtrack on foot the two or three passed-up stops. I recall now, and not without a fair amount of pride and amusement, the older I got, the more stops I required.

Until today, I figured I had outgrown this adolescent behavior long ago. However, my luncheon encounter at the Lantern raised new doubts, as well as that old, familiar occurrence. I was back on the bus again. I'm grateful my Burberry trench coat served double duty, concealing the embarrassing reaction to my sophomoric relapse.

Huddled groups of smokers dotted the small plaza at the building entrance as they grabbed the last few precious drags before reentering their legislated smoke-free work environments. I wondered if she'd be returning to her office straight from lunch. Within minutes, I had my answer. I spotted her paused at the crosswalk on the far side of Sixth Avenue.

A windblown newspaper page wrapped itself around my shoe. I shook it free, and it continued its gusty journey. I noticed as she waited for the light to change, the self-possessed way she stood as if she was defying the city's traffic department to keep her waiting longer than necessary.

The signal flashed WALK, and I pushed my hands deeper into the pockets of my Burberry.

She saw me. I was sure. My chest tightened while my mind raced through a hastily prepared opening line. My schoolboy anxiety puzzled me. Hell, I'd picked up women before, many times: in singles bars, on the street with a friendly smile, on planes, buses, and trains, even on the subway once, always with great success and none leading to anything longer than a one-nighter.

There was one exception. Last year, an encounter on Fire Island with Maryann from Citibank. It exploded as a hot summer romance, which, for a brief time, I judged could become serious. But it ended in the frigid reality of a New York City winter. I recovered within a week. "Hardly missed a beat," I bragged to my friends in my office.

Someone once told me I had an edge. They said that because of my non-threatening looks and Bible-belt demeanor, I'm able to defuse any suspicion of my real intentions. I don't know if it's true, although one thing is certain. Women trust me. The result enhances my single lifestyle, a proverbial cornucopia of sexual liaisons since moving to the city ten years ago. The recruiter, during career week at Southern Methodist University, covered the advertising agency's fast-track management training program in depth, but somehow neglected to mention that perk.

As the woman approached, I tried to dismiss my edginess. I had a feeling this would not be just another pickup. Her step was brisk and her path direct. Her long hair tossed about in the changing wind. She appeared taller and more mature than she did in the coffee shop. There was an arrogance to her stride. Her bounce reminded me of the morning I watched SMU's homecoming queen make her way across the grassy campus quadrangle after a steamy night in my room.

She reached me and I recited my rehearsed gambit. "Are you aware you look exactly like Melina Kanakaredes of CSI?"

She struck a hand-on-hip pose. "Is that why you're waiting for me? To tell me that?"

I sensed I had offended her, except I caught sight of a small grin forming. "No, not for that, but the resemblance sure got my attention at the Lantern." She was smiling now, and I felt more confident. The butterflies disappeared as they always did after the initial body contact on the opening kickoff.

"Well, the name's Victoria, not Melina, and since we're working neighbors," she said, holding out her business card, "call me later about dinner tomorrow night."

Unprepared as I was for her directness, her words required a moment to register. When the irony of the role reversal penetrated, I exploded with laughter. "How do you know I'm free tomorrow night? I'm called Will, by the way." I removed a business card from my inside pocket and handed it to her.

She looked at my name. "I don't know, William Andrew McMillan, but I'm free, and if you are too, call me later today and we'll arrange to get together for dinner." Her voice was firm, with no trace of awkwardness. She could have been trying to negotiate a court date with a rival counselor. "Sorry, I have to run," she said. "I have a two o'clock meeting. Call me, Will. Bye, again." I stared as she disappeared into the whirl of the building's revolving doors.

* * *

Victoria Harte selected the place; a small, tony French bistro in the East Village called Le Giraffe. She insisted on making the reservation herself. I arrived at the arranged time and the maître d' greeted me by name.

"Ah-ha, Monsieur McMillan," he intoned with a familiarity that rang an alarm in my head. My hand went to my right rump where I kept my wallet and American Express Gold Card. Victoria had warned she might be a little late, so I elected to wait at the small bar near the door.

"Something to drink?" the tiny, mustached barman asked.

"Yes, please, a Heineken."

I faced the dining area to absorb the surroundings. A pattern of watercolor scenes of the African veldt papered the walls: a herd of spindle-legged giraffes romping across the barren plain, lion prides yawning under the white afternoon sun, spotted cheetahs in full stride through the brush in hot pursuit of a frightened, swift-footed impala. It was as if I'd walked onto the set of a National Geographic television special.

Victoria arrived three Heinekens late. She floated through the restaurant's entrance, a regal image, unaware of her tardiness. I wobbled down from my stool to take her coat. Slipping it from her shoulders, I gazed down at a chic, black chiffon cocktail dress, which I learned later was an original Givenchy. A low-cut bodice displayed her well-rounded, buttery-smooth, freckled cleavage, an attractive backdrop for a string of pure white pearls. Her elegance staggered me. I was glad I'd selected a blue pinstripe suit, my best Paul Stuart model, instead of the sports jacket and slacks I had set out when I arrived home. I was certain casual attire was something Victoria wore only to bed.

"Ah, mademoiselle, eet iz zo nice to zee you again," the maître d' purred while he escorted us to a series of two-seaters along one side of the restaurant.

Victoria selected the outside chair. I squeezed through the space between tables onto a hard, leather banquette lining the wall, happy not to stare at the wallpaper menagerie throughout dinner.

The maître d' placed two menus on the table in front of us. "Perhaps an apéritif before ordering?" he suggested.

I looked at Victoria.

"Yes, Jean-Paul. Lillet, if you please, with a lemon twist. Will, what would you like?"

"Another Heineken, please," I said.

"Oh, Will, not a beer. We're going French tonight."

I couldn't miss her disapproving tone.

"Have what I'm having, Lillet. You'll enjoy it, I promise."

I nodded, and the efficient Jean-Paul was off.

Dinner went well. The selected courses of French fare at Le Giraffe, orchestrated with perfection by Victoria, were a delicious experience. Our whispered conversation across the small table revealed many shared interests: authors, exotic places, sports, and the theater.

She confessed she had never married. Raised in Hartford, Connecticut, the daughter of an insurance company president, she spent her undergraduate years at Oberlin College, calling it the bedrock of twenty-first-century liberalism. She moved to New York to get her LLD from Columbia Law the same year I graduated from SMU.

* * *

Victoria entered the taxi ahead of me, giving the driver instructions before I could get in. She directed the cabbie to take us to 625 Central Park West.

The little Pakistani squinted into his rearview mirror as though he was trying to read her lips, turned, and shook his head with a questioning expression

Victoria added, "The West Side Drive might be the quickest way." It got results. Our taxi ride uptown was swift.

"Where are we going? I thought we'd have a nightcap somewhere, like The Oak Room of the Plaza," I said, trying to retain the ritzy tone of the evening. The Oak Room was out of my league unless I was with an agency client; however, I was not eager to end the date this early.

"I have a better idea. We can have a nightcap at my apartment." She moved closer to entwine herself around my arm for our first real physical contact. "I have a bottle of wonderful French cognac to warm us up. How's that sound?"

She was offering me the first opportunity of the evening to make a choice. "Just fine," I said, "but how about I pay for the taxi? I'm bothered you picked up the tab at the restaurant."

"Oh, Will, don't be," she cooed. "I invited you, remember? Next time, your treat. Okay?" She snuggled her chin to my shoulder as she spoke and pressed her thigh against mine. I could only manage a soft groan.

The taxi pulled to a stop at the entrance of an up-scale cooperative on Central Park West whose monogrammed awning traveled from the curb to the front door.

"Good evening, Miss Harte," the doorman said as he opened the cab door. He held it until we exited and rushed ahead to push open the heavy glass door to the building's paneled lobby. We rode the east wing elevator in silence to the twenty-second floor.

"Goodnight, Miss Harte," the elevator man said in a tone a bit too knowing.

We emerged into a small foyer with two doors. The first had SERVICE stenciled on the face. We entered through the second one into a high-ceilinged, wood-paneled, richly decorated world I knew existed only from the movies. We took our cognac to the terrace and watched the lights of New York City blink over Central Park. I found it easy to ignore the chilly night air.

* * *

"Just let yourself out," she told me in the morning as I dressed and prepared to leave her apartment. "It's Saturday, and I'm going to rest awhile in bed." Grinning, she said, "You wore me out."

I bent over her naked outline to whisper goodbye, and my heart raced when I looked down at her sleepy face. Sunlight made its way through the slats of the drawn blinds and etched her cheeks with a pattern of lines. I craved to get back under the sheets with her. She rolled over, stretched her arms, grasped me around the neck, pulled me down to a long, loving kiss, and breathed in my ear, "It was super, wasn't it, Will? Then again, I knew you'd be."

"Vikki, I've never met anyone like you. When do I see you again? When should I call?"

"Toward the end of the week, okay? I may have to be in D.C. for a few days."

* * *

In order not to appear eager, I waited until Friday morning. "I'm sorry, Mr. McMillan," her secretary said. "She's out of town and won't return until Monday." I left my office number even though Victoria had my business card. I asked the secretary to repeat it back to me.

On Monday, I called again. "Miss Harte is with a client and can't be disturbed."

The third and fourth times were much the same. I let a week go by and called again. "Sorry, Mr. McMillan. Miss Harte is in court this morning. I'll tell her you called."

This afternoon, following my fifth call and two hours of introspective window gazing, I made a different call.

"Hey, Maryann. It's Will. . . . Yes, it's me. . . . Yes, I'm fine, thanks. . . . Uh-huh, that's why I'm calling. The guys want me to go in on a house this summer. That's right, Fire Island. Are you considering going out there again? You are? Hey, great! Maybe we can . . . ."

I AIN'T EATIN'

Frank Brancuso watched his widowed mother give the eye to the tubby, smiling Sicilian proprietor as the man strutted among tables of diners. He gave off the aura of a grower of rare grapes inspecting his treasured vineyards.

My mother, always the flirt, Frank thought. No wonder she enjoys coming here. The only four-star Italian restaurant between Smithtown and Port Jefferson, it was his usual choice for holidays and special occasions. And the chef's beef bracciole was something else, better than his mother's, although he would never say it aloud.

The host passed their table and acknowledged Sarah's fluttering lids with a courtly nod. With her well-grooved frown restored, Sarah turned back to her son and daughter-in-law.

"Mary and saints! You drive all the way out here to take me to dinner for my birthday, and the only thing you can talk about is me selling the house. You should have telephoned, saved you the long trip. I don't want to go back to Manhattan. Can't you understand that?"

Marie smiled one of those smiles that said, We're concerned about you. Honest! Her deep-set eyes squinted below her middle-aged, rumpled brow.

Sarah continued her protest, firing her self-justifying points with machine-gun speed. "Moving back to the city makes little sense. Anything I need, I got right here. A boy who cuts the grass. Mrs. Coogan across the street takes me to church. I can walk to Stop'n' Shop half a mile down the highway—don't worry, I always stay near the shoulder. I want company, I go next door to my new neighbors, a Pakistani family. Moved in last month. Nice people, too. They even taught me a few Pakistani words."

"Look, Mama," Frank said, jumping in when she paused and drew a breath, "what if you became ill, or, God forbid, you fall and break something? Who would know? Mama, you're eighty-six. These things can happen."

"My neighbors call me every once in a while," she said, as though she found an irrefutable rebuttal.

"But it takes me two hours to drive from the city. If there was an emergency, I'd never get here in time." He rolled his eyes while shaking his head. The fat candle flickering in the center of the table drew his attention. Hot, multi-colored rivers of melting wax worked down the sides, the flame sure to disappear before the next seating finished their salad. He hoped it wasn't an omen.

Marie broke the silence. "You'll love the apartment, Sarah. You have a short walk to all the stores, and there's a senior citizen center four blocks away."

Sarah glared at her daughter-in-law. "Who the hell needs to be around all those old people? And I've seen the apartment, Marie," she snapped, "even before you!"

Frank made a face at his wife. Cool it; don't play her game, it said.

* * *

Frank had moved into his one-bedroom unit seven years ago after quitting suburbia and a twenty-year marriage that had turned sour. The luxury high-rise spanned Lexington Avenue between 36th and 37th Streets. Four years later, when the building ownership converted it from a rental to a cooperative, Frank purchased his apartment at the insider's price.

The lobby's new plush, red carpeting smelled clean, and the wood-paneled walls buffed to a warm, rich luster shone under the ceiling's recessed lighting. The building's three shifts of uniformed doormen whipped open and banged shut taxi doors around the clock while they guarded the portal of this up-scale co-op.

Located in the Murray Hill area of Manhattan, the neighborhood afforded him a quick subway ride to his Wall Street law firm and easy access to theaters, restaurants, and all the other pleasures his single status accorded him. He enjoyed his lifestyle until a year ago when, in Sarah's words, "One of Frank's partners couldn't leave well enough alone and introduced him to Marie."

He eased into this new relationship like a sore foot into an old shoe. In the beginning, Marie would stay the night from time to time, leaving changes of clothing and a few toiletries. The frequency of their dating increased, as did her overnights. Eventually, she took over one closet and shared his bed more often than she slept on her own.

"My mother grew horns and a tail," Frank would say whenever he described that first weekend he brought Marie out to Sarah's house to introduce her. Soon after their arrival, he announced their plan to marry, and the next two days proceeded downhill into a moody abyss.

While Marie was off examining the summer sunset over the back fence, Sarah took the opportunity to lecture her son. "What's the matter, Frank, you can't stand being on your own? It isn't hard, you know. What's the rush? You're hardly over your first marriage. Take time before you jump back into the fire," then adding after a beat, "By the way, Frank, I never cared much for your instant compatibility."

Ah, the real thorn, he thought. "Mama, when are you going to stop treating me like I was still a kid? I'm turning fifty soon!" He raked his fingers through his thick, dark hair, salted at the temples with gray. It pleased him his face displayed none of the usual age lines—a gift of his Italian heritage—and people often took him for ten years younger. "For Pete's sake, Mama, I don't want to spend the rest of my life alone."

Two months later, he married Marie, and they went into contract on a sizeable two-bedroom layout in a cooperative right down the street from his one-bedroom unit.

* * *

The waiter appeared to top off champagne glasses, whispering an offer of *zabaglione*, a dessert reserved for favored patrons. When he departed, Sarah resumed her argument.

"Now, you're asking me to move back to a way of life me and your papa left over thirty years ago. What for? To be wet-nursed by you two? Looked out for myself all my life, I have. I could teach them women's lib people a thing or two."

Frank flashed back to Sarah's long diatribe on that movement the year of his divorce. "A bunch of wimps," she called them.

Sarah continued, "Survived my first husband, and later your papa after he died. What's that tell you? Damn! I can get along very nicely, thank you, by myself and living in my own home." She let out a deep sigh and reached for her champagne glass.

"Listen, Mama, I don't mean to sound cruel. Sooner or later, there comes a point where you're not able to manage on your own. Isn't this arrangement a lot better than a cold, indifferent nursing home?" Marie's head nodded in support.

Sarah kept silent, staring into the fluted champagne glass.

"It's a seller's market now," Marie said, attempting to soften the mood. "You would get top dollar for the house."

"Makes no never mind," Sarah said without turning toward her daughter-in-law. "I lived in my house for a long time. We put down our roots there—literally. Frank, you remember your father seeded the first lawn, planted the first willows and dogwoods, and had the walkway lined with juniper bushes?"

Frank winced at the last reference. Six months ago, Sarah had called to say she was having the bushes removed. "Damned things grew so high, I can't see to the sidewalk," his mother told him. He said it was irrational. She should have them trimmed, and digging them up would ruin the grass and the appearance of the house. None of it mattered. Sarah hired someone—a local handyman—and up came the bushes.

She never owned up to the real reason for removing them, but he knew. She worried about someone sneaking up to the front door, hiding behind the juniper's overgrowth, and she wouldn't spot him until it was too late. "These days, with all the crime in the area," she confessed to him on the phone last summer, "you can't be too careful. The neighborhood's changed a lot in recent years."

Over *zabaglione, espresso,* and *anisette,* Frank reminded her of that concern—several times.

* * *

Sarah stood in the open doorway watching the eight-wheel behemoth edge out of the driveway, maneuver a sharp left, and turn up the road. The giant van with Garibaldi Brothers-

Four emblazoned on the side panels, back panels, header panel, and above the peak of the skinny driver's baseball cap, lumbered out of view with the few remaining possessions she had fought hard to keep.

"Garibaldi Brothers-Four," she voiced aloud. "Sounds like a circus act." She smiled at her own humor. "Wonder if they even got it tattooed on their butts."

"What did you say?" Frank asked, his voice echoing from within the open trunk of his car.

"Nothing."

Her diminutive five feet had reached only to the young driver's shoulder when she cozied up to him to ask if he was really one of the brothers. "More'n likely, he's the runt of the litter," she later whispered to Frank.

Sarah looked at her son, his head stuck deep into the car trunk, his body struggling to rearrange the loaded contents. "Frank," she hollered, "if all the furniture isn't strapped down good, everything's going flying when they try to make the turn at the top of the hill."

"Don't worry about it, Mama. They did a good job."

"Yeah, well, with so little left, I don't want to lose more in the move." The van was only half-full. She wondered why they had sent such a large truck.

The movers loaded the furniture in less than two hours, taking only the pieces Frank determined would fit in the small one-bedroom, one-bath co-op. The rest of the furniture, after he'd arm-twisted her weeks before, he put into the garage sale.

Her hands smoothed the folds of her faded housedress, while she admired her reflection in the glass of the propped-open storm door. With a self-conscious gesture, she brushed back a few gray strands of her short coiffure. Her hair glistened in the morning sunlight, though not as radiant as when, in her thirties, her waist-length, rich chestnut hair was the envy of both sides of the family.

Sarah pictured herself nestling baby Frank on her lap under her cascading locks, pretending she couldn't find him, and he would shake with giggles. Funny, she mused, sometimes I can't remember what I had for breakfast, yet these nurturing visits from almost fifty years ago appear as if they just happened.

The momentary recall of the past returned her to a time when life was manageable and within her control. "Damn it!" she shouted. "I don't need to be wet-nursed by you and Marie. I'm staying here."

Frank shot back a glare before he placed the last carton of kitchenware, china, and glassware on the rear seat of the car, items Sarah would not trust to the Garibaldi Brothers. "Mama, we're not moving you in with us. You'll have your own place, independent, right up the street."

* * *

The movers left the apartment, and Sarah was relieved to see all the furniture fit. The dimensions of the rooms and their contoured walls dictated where each piece went. She had forgotten about their odd shapes, having visited Frank only once during the years he lived there. Sarah had arrived in the city to attend the funeral of her childhood friend, Lilly Bogart, and spent the night on the sofa bed. She refused when Frank suggested she take his bed.

Growing up in the Yorkville section of Manhattan, she remembered, Lilly was the best dancer of all her girlfriends. Oh, was she popular with the boys, she recalled, the ones we would meet at all those ballroom dance places around the city. Sarah and Lilly had remained friends for seventy-five years, staying in touch until her friend ended up in that God-awful nursing home in Brooklyn. Poor Lilly.

"Mama, you okay?"

"What? Oh . . . oh, yeah, sure," she said, opening her eyes. "I was just resting." She pushed to her feet and reached back to fluff the sofa pillows.

"You're going to love it here, Mama, I promise," Frank said as he stripped the masking tape from the first carton of dishes. "All the shopping you'll need, right down the street on Third Avenue. No more half-mile walks."

Sarah glanced around the room, appraising its appearance. Everything in place, well, it surprised her how cozy it felt. She walked into the tiny kitchen and bent over the stainless sink. With meticulous care, she rinsed and dried each piece of mismatched china as Frank unwrapped it from its newspaper protection. She carefully stacked everything—plates of various sizes and patterns (only two from her original set left), cups with and without ears, saucers, and seven Welch's grape jelly glasses—onto the bottom shelf of the cabinet.

She could have used the other two upper shelves if Frank hadn't thrown her step stool into the garage sale at the house. Now, Sarah had no way of reaching above the first shelf unless she dragged over a chair and stood on it. She doubted she had the muscle and balance for such a gymnastic feat. She remembered him warning, "I don't want you climbing on things."

Frank stuffed the discarded newspaper into the emptied packing boxes and carried them out the door and down the hallway to the incinerator room. Before he returned, Sarah slipped out of the kitchen, leaving the water running.

"Mama, where are you?" he called upon re-entering the apartment.

"Move the highboy over here," she said from the bedroom. "Don't seem right where it is."

He arrived and saw her pointing to the spot where she wanted the twelve-drawer dresser moved. He threw up his hands. She had indicated the area in front of the lone window.

"Mama, you put it there, it'll block any light coming in."

"That's okay. I don't want people looking in at night. We're too close to those houses across the yard. They can see right into the window."

Her second-floor bedroom faced north, toward the rear of a row of brownstones lining the south side of 37th Street. The view looked down on a tree-shaded remnant of a more pastoral era—a mixture of broken cement patios, dried-out weeds once passing for lawns, and fallen down, wooden-stockade fences. One hundred feet of nostalgia was all that separated her from her neighbors.

"Mama, there's Venetian blinds in every window in the apartment. Simply lower them at night."

"I don't care. Move it there anyway."

"Let's leave it where it is for a while," he said, sounding like a pediatrician speaking to a young patient. "Later, if you insist on moving it, we'll get a couple of the building porters to come up and wrestle with it. I'll put my back out if I try to do it now." He pulled on the cord of the Venetian blind to lower it and said, "Meantime, close them this way."

Sarah watched, keeping one eye on the demonstration while shooting a suspicious glance at the wall of windows of the old brownstones that mirrored the late afternoon sun.

* * *

He could hear the voice of Chris Wallace on "Fox News Sunday" in the background when she answered the phone. It was more than a month since the move and well into the test of her ability to cope with urban living.

"How about a trip up to Central Park this afternoon? It's a beautiful day, and Marie and I are in the mood for some fresh air after lunch."

Over breakfast, he reflected on Sarah's daily half-mile trek to Stop 'n' Shop, now replaced by a short stroll to D'Agostino's Supermarket on Third Avenue. Relieved she was no longer required to dodge highway traffic to shop for food, he had to admit the old routine provided a form of cardiovascular exercise. An afternoon outing through the city's zoo would be a good thing. He suggested it to Marie over coffee, adding Sarah no doubt hadn't visited there since his childhood.

"I'm sorry, Frank, not today."

"You're sure? It'd be a chance to stretch your legs, and get the old circulation flowing."

"You go ahead. I'm going to line my bureau drawers."

"Alright. Which reminds me, did you have the porters move the dresser?"

Her response surprised him. "No, no. I decided to let it stay put."

The following evening he called again. He counted nine rings. On the tenth, she picked up.

"Hello."

"Mama, what's the matter? What took you so long to answer?"

"Frank?"

"Yeah, of course. You expecting someone else? You okay?"

"Why wouldn't I be?"

"Well, you sound strange. Where were you, the bathroom?"

He heard the phone drop on the desk. A long stretch of silence followed.

"For heaven's sake, Mama, where are you? What's going on?" he yelled.

She returned and said, "Sorry, Frank, I forgot to shut the window. What were you saying?"

Patience, he told himself for an even dozen times this month. "Look, Marie's holding dinner for you. You were supposed to be here by six-thirty. Monday and Wednesday, remember?"

She mumbled a reply that he missed.

"Mama, what did you say?"

"Yeah, I just remembered something you said when you were six or seven, when you noticed something on your plate you didn't like."

"What's that?"

"I ain't eatin'."

"What?"

"I ain't eatin'. You said it often, and that's what I'm trying to tell you. I'm not coming to dinner. I ain't eatin'."

The chortle came from the back of her throat, low and raspy. It was unmistakable. He heard the sound when he was a teenager, at family gatherings during the penny-ante poker games her brother-in-law always started. Her eyes would crinkle and dart around the table with a mischievous expression of triumph. Then she'd laugh and reveal a full house or four of a kind.

"Well, you have to eat something." He was certain her refrigerator contained little more than a few Stouffers' frozen dinners. "Did you make yourself some dinner?"

"Yes, sure, I ate something."

He doubted it, but he decided not to argue. "Okay, I'll tell Marie. Wednesday night, then?"

"What?"

"I said we'll see you Wednesday night—for dinner, right?"

"Maybe."

* * *

Wednesday evening, at Marie's insistence, Frank traveled from work straight to Sarah's apartment to check on her. "Perhaps her memory is faltering, and she's too embarrassed to admit it," Marie said.

Tom, the day-shift doorman, was at the building entrance on the southeast corner of 36th Street. He was closing the door of a yellow cab when Frank reached the green awning.

"Evening, Mr. Brancuso," the man said. A standard, snappy military salute accompanied the greeting. "If you're looking for your mother, she's gone out."

"Oh? I guess she's already waiting in my lobby."

"I didn't see her heading down that way. She was walking with that nice old gentleman, you know, the one that lives around the corner, one of those brownstones. They were going up toward Fifth Avenue."

"An old gentleman? . . . brownstone ? . . . toward Fifth Avenue?" He repeated the words to be sure he heard them correctly.

"Yes, sir, around five-thirty."

Frank squinted westward into the disappearing sun. When the realization blossomed, a smile formed. "She probably left the blinds up too long."

"What's that, sir?"

"Oh, nothing. Thanks, Tom." Turning toward Third Avenue, he started down the sloping street and recognized his step had developed a slight bounce.

RUBYRED AND PARSHOOTER

This stage of Junior Boylan's young life was static, moving very little off-center since his graduation from high school five years ago. Treading water both professionally and emotionally never worried him. Not until that night, when Providence, the divinity that shapes our end, urged him to turn on his computer.

"Time to go to the candy store," Junior said aloud as he typed in his password to the computer-dating website, eSexysingles.com. The home page flickered to life across his new flat screen monitor and welcomed PARSHOOTER to this haven of hope-searching members. He opened to the library page of female candidates who matched the thirty-six traits of his on-file personality profile. So many choices, so many scores his mind rumbled, as he scrolled through the array of familiar faces and bodies, a fair amount he'd already sampled.

Junior stopped at a new entry, one he hadn't seen before. Screen name RUBYRED. He brought up her résumé page and clicked on the first of the posted small photos. Her round, cherubic face filled the enlarged screen, her blue eyes staring out above a painted red smile. A full mane of firecracker red hair framed RUBYRED'S accented, blushed-on cheeks, completing for anyone old enough to remember, an anachronistic picture from a 1940s Vargas Girl calendar.

Junior reduced the image to its original postage-stamp size and moved the cursor to her next photo, enlarged it with a click, this one posed in girlie-magazine fashion. Seated on the end of a diving board, she wore a bikini that looked like someone had drawn the two-piece cover-up with a sharp number-two pencil. Her endowments leaped off the page despite the adoring white poodle perched on her lap and licking her chin. "Another winner," he declared as he clicked the wink button to send his message of interest.

It was close to midnight, his eyelids heavy from watching Monday Night Football on the twenty-one-inch TV set in his one-room apartment above his parents' garage. No time to read RUBYRED's profile description before crawling into bed. Besides, he was certain most of the things they listed— all that crap about long walks on the beach, leisure suppers in candlelit cafes, bestseller books, and classical music—was pure invention. He never doubted the women he winked at electronically all harbored the same prurient interests he did. His almost-perfect success rate did nothing to discourage that belief.

It was Junior's turn to open the pro shop at seven. He needed his rest for a nine-thirty golf lesson with the lovely Mrs. Baumeister, whose bra size, he joked with his head pro, matched her handicap: forty. Let's see if RUBYRED answers my wink with an email, he thought, as he shut down the computer.

* * *

In the morning, Mike O'Shea, the Oak Tree Golf and Country Club cart barn supervisor, asked him, "Junior, wadda ya wanna be when you grow up?" Junior had finished describing his latest internet find to his former boss, taking pains to include accurate details of the diving board picture.

The Irishman ran his stubby fingers through his white Brillo-like hair. The thumb and forefingers of his other hand, hooked under his wide belt, struggled to pull up his khaki trousers over his bulbous belly. His faded Oak Tree-monogrammed golf shirt reeked of Clorox and stretched beyond the limits intended by the manufacturer. It was clear Mike's rumpled expression was one of disapproval.

"Junior, you need to stop wasting your life chasing girls and playing golf. You should be thinking about your future. Mind you, lad, there's not much opportunity in this business unless you become a head pro. Or you hone your game enough to make it on the tour. I mean, after I landed here from Killarney and took up with the postal system, I had a decent run for twenty-five years before getting into this job. This country club business is for retirees looking for stress-free work. Or youngsters who want free golf."

This fatherly connection saved Junior from termination the many times he stretched the man's patience. His job during those four summers working in the cart barn during high school always hung on a thread.

After graduation, Junior moved into the golf shop as a full-time sales associate behind the counter. Three years later, he began as an assistant teaching pro, despite not being certified.

"But you need to be in the PGA program," the head pro had told him, "or I won't let you teach. That's the deal." Junior signed up with a loan from his father to help pay the tuition, and he passed the Playing Ability Test the next month. "Finished three shots under for the two rounds," he boasted to Mike the following day.

The old Irishman continued with his admonition. "You hear what I'm saying, son?"

"I don't know, Mike. I always fantasized about making a career in golf . . . become a head pro someday. They make top money, for sure."

"True, boyo, at certain swanky clubs they do. You understand, once you start down that path, you face a long, hard grind. You got the stuff for the journey?"

"Well, yeah, I got the game."

"That's nice, son, except there's more to the PGA program than your playing ability. You've been studying in it, what, two years? And you've only completed the first phase of the bookwork? Sports bars and chasin' women take precedence over learning, do they? You realize they give you three years to finish the book part; otherwise, you go back to square one."

"I know that. I'm working on the book whenever I can. Hell, I already know a lot about running the cart barn."

Mike scowled. "Lad, when are you gonna pull your socks up and get real? What are you waiting for, some fairy to come sprinkle you with magic dust to jump-start you?"

The young man had always accepted Mike's reproaches without challenge. He knew the cart barn supervisor's motive was in his best interest. Despite everything, a change in Junior's mindset was beyond his self-control.

Junior was spoiled. His six-foot athletic frame, thick, tousled hair, undeniable good looks, and natural charm endeared him to the Oak Tree membership, to whom he doled out his playing knowledge through many golf lessons. The younger set of female club members coveted his teaching times. His lessons rarely ended on the practice tee.

RUBYRED answered his wink the next evening. "Let's meet for a drink," she suggested, adding that she hoped it could be an enlightening meeting—her words. Junior wasn't sure what she meant, but that didn't discourage his imagination from taking flight.

"A nice quiet place where we can talk," was how she ended the communique. He realized that eliminated his typical sports bar hangouts. Those haunts, with their saturated beer aroma and high levels of testosterone, were suitable for meeting and connecting with people who were into the NFL, NBA, MLB, NHL, NASCAR, and sometimes the PGA. The noise level produced by the watchers of these multi-televised sporting events drowned out anything resembling a social conversation. No, a sports bar was not the place to meet RUBYRED for a drink. Something in his gut told him this date would be different. He emailed her, selecting the bar at the local Holiday Inn, and she answered, confirming Wednesday evening after work was fine.

* * *

The Holiday Inn, an unfamiliar, older social atmosphere, was busy when Junior entered. He glanced around at the more formal attire and was glad he had opted to wear his new blue blazer. He climbed on a stool near the end of the long bar, close to the door where he would watch for RUBYRED, confident he could pick her out, even with clothes on.

The Inn's watering hole hosted a few visiting sales representatives on the prowl, and a couple of homemakers trying to act innocent while their unmarried companions scoped out possibilities. Mostly locals made up the Inn's Happy Hour, a regular stop before going home after work.

The soundless TV set, tuned to the stock market channel, hung over the back of the bar. A low chatter from patrons created the room's only noise. Looking around, Junior became convinced he'd made the right call when he ruled out the roar of a sports hangout for this first date with RUBYRED.

"You want a glass or just the bottle?" the bartender asked as he set down the imported beer Junior ordered.

Junior hesitated. They gave no one that option at those high-testosterone places he frequented, where everyone sucked beer from the bottle. He considered the impression that would make on RUBYRED. "Yeah, glass is fine. A frosted mug if you got it?"

"Yes sir, we can do that," the barman replied.

"PARSHOOTER?"

The soft voice reached the back of Junior's neck, nestling there while his brain processed the sound of his screen name. He had taken a sip of beer and placed the mug back on the coaster as the voice reached him. Junior did a slow turn in her direction. The blaze of red hair, backlit by a white halo of light, almost blinded him. He blinked and squinted several times before he responded.

"RUBYRED?"

She stepped closer, out of the dazzling effect of the setting sun streaming through the windows behind her, and slowly came into focus. Her smile beamed at him, intimate as if she was greeting an old friend. Her Kelly-green blazer set off her thick, textured red hair like a fire alarm. The yellow cotton shirt under her jacket, buttoned at the neck, sported a subtle, stitched design on the collar. A pair of form-fitting khaki slacks covered her legs, the curvy ones he remembered trailing off the end of the diving board. She wore black ankle boots, turned up at the toes, and made of a smooth, satiny fabric.

"Junior?"

She knew his real name.

"North Tampa Central High School, right?"

She knew that too.

"I suspected there was something familiar in the bio of yours . . . six feet, sandy-blond hair, plays golf, loves the Dolphins and Marlins, hates math and studying, and loves Elmore Leonard's novels." Her voice was clear and articulated.

Junior sprung from his stool, almost falling into her before he regained his balance. Her full size reached the middle of his chest, and her shapely figure was everything the photos on his computer promised. The luster of her skin was pale pink, and when she thrust out her hand, he took it into both of his and held it as he would a piece of fragile porcelain.

"You know me?" He was clueless. Nothing familiar came to him, not from the pictures on her pages, not from seeing her now in person.

She continued to smile with the confidence of someone about to reveal a secret. "I guess you don't remember me. Ginger Tibsen. Geometry, and American history. We were in those classes together in our senior year at Central."

The name Ginger Tibsen sounded familiar, but it baffled him. He remembered only a girl with reddish hair, a ruddy complexion, a dumpy body, and a nerdy personality who sat in front of him during both courses. She was smart as hell and aced every test as if someone had provided her the answers in advance. But he could not recall a time when he noticed her outside the classroom.

They remained standing until he reached back for the stool next to him and pulled it out. "Well, damn, let's sit down while I figure this out. What are you drinking?"

She climbed onto the padded seat and said, "Something diet, please. A Coke is fine."

"Nothing stronger?"

"No, thank you."

Motioning to the bartender, he flashed back to the photo on the diving board. "So you have a dog—a poodle?"

"My folks thought I needed company. They gave him to me last Christmas."

He wanted to jump right to the question of her physical transformation but thought twice. How do you approach the subject with tact? Ask, hey, how did you morph from being a pudgy nerd to a gorgeous fox? Uh-uh.

The barman returned. "A Diet Coke for the lady, and I'll have another Becks," Junior said without turning away from her. He pushed the empty mug forward to trade it for a frosted one. "Well, let's see, now," he said. "How long has it been? Three, four years? You graduated the same year I did, didn't you?"

"Yes. Five years ago."

Junior's gaze continued to fix on her face. "Five years? Where the hell did the time go?"

"It goes by fast, for sure. We shouldn't waste it."

The bartender approached with the bottle of Becks and two mugs.

Ginger raised her Diet Coke and extended it toward Junior. "Here's to old friends, and may the best day of your past be the worst day of your future." She took a sip and placed it on the coaster. "Want to tell me what's kept you busy since graduation?"

"Why don't you go first? My five years can't be anywhere near as interesting as yours," he said, his mind returning to her physical change.

"Alright. Promise to stop me if you become bored?"

Junior repositioned himself to permit him to face her straight-on and placed his shoes on the rung of her stool below her dangling feet. "I doubt it will happen," he said.

Ginger smiled and began. "After high school, I enrolled in Dowling College upstate, majoring in philosophy."

"My impression was everyone who went there majored in basket weaving or surfing," he said, referencing an old joke about Dowling's supposed easy curriculum.

She ignored his interruption and continued. "When I got there, my freshman-year roommate was into a rigid physical fitness routine. In self-defense, I got involved. After four years, I not only graduated with honors in my philosophy major, I did it with a new body. Which, I'm proud to say, made the 'Girls of Florida Colleges' edition of *Playboy Magazine* in my senior year.

"No shit!" As soon as Junior said it, he slapped his hand over his mouth trying to stuff back his words.

"No problem. It surprised the faculty and administration too. They came close to suspending me. I almost didn't graduate. My folks supported my decision to do the photoshoot. They argued with the college that they should allow me to receive my degree because of my outstanding academic record. The Dean relented, although he was none too happy."

Junior remained motionless, staring, mesmerized. If she had been a sports bar pickup, the concept of posing for a *Playboy* layout would have been easy to grasp. He had a problem making the connection with a smart Ginger Tibsen, a college honors graduate. He shook his head. "What in the world made you do it? Pose for the magazine, I mean. I'm not being critical, you understand."

Ginger's angelic face belied her answer. "I did it because they asked, and because I could. I worked long and hard those four years to develop into who I am now, and I had no reason to hide it. Should I have?"

"No, no . . . jeez, no. You know what they say. If you got it, flaunt it."

Junior's thoughts drifted, weighing the stark contrast of their lives. Ginger was sure of herself and in charge. Unlike most girls her age, she knew who she was, and was not shy about the image she created. He couldn't imagine her behaving any other way. She had a dream, went for it full bore, and made it happen. "My God, I think I love you."

She laughed.

The bartender's head swiveled around, and Junior caught the smirk. "Just kidding," he said, trying to salvage his dignity. He turned back to her and said, "Yeah, well, what I mean is, wow! I envy you. You do any more posing . . . ah, modeling, that is?"

"Only in sweatpants and tee shirts at Gold's Gym. I'm a physical fitness trainer there. After college, I considered ways to use my philosophy degree. There wasn't much opportunity except for teaching. Right now, I'm working on my certification as a physical therapist."

The word therapist triggered a medical image of someone on an uphill career path toward a goal requiring study, dedication, and total commitment. Junior wondered how much time it would leave her for a social life.

"Now, your turn," she said. "Tell me, what have you been up to since Central?"

He leaned back against the bar and rested his elbow. A sense of awkwardness seeped in when he focused on the past five years. "You sure you want to hear about it? I mean, it ain't *Gulliver's Travels*." Ginger's expression reminded him of Mike O'Toole's when he got into one of his parental moods.

"What happened after graduation," she asked, "when Florida State offered you a golf scholarship? Why didn't you accept it?"

"You kiddin' me? How the hell do you know about that?"

"Class gossip, nothing more."

He didn't look away.

"It was true, then?"

"Yeah. Anyway, my SAT scores sucked. And I was familiar with a few of the guys on State's squad. My golf game then? Not even close to their level."

Junior realized it was the first time he admitted that to anyone other than Mike O'Toole. He searched Ginger's face for a reaction and found none.

"I worked in the cart barn at the Oak Tree Golf Country Club during summer vacations in high school. When I graduated, the golf shop supervisor there offered me a full-time job as a sales associate. Figured it could be a good first step. I teach golf now, except I'm not certified. After I complete the PGA program, I'll be certified as a golf pro," he said as he flagged the bartender.

"You really want that, don't you?"

He stiffened as he shot her a puzzled expression. "Hey, I only had two. I can handle a—"

Ginger cut him off. "Not the beer, you goof. I meant the program. To finish and become a PGA professional?"

"Sorry," he said, allowing his shoulders to relax.

Ginger smiled and waited.

"Well, yeah, sure. More than anything." He felt his chest swell when he spoke the words. The bartender arrived. "Two more of the same," Junior ordered.

"Not for me, thanks. I still have a little left here," Ginger said and lifted the mug to her cheek as if to verify her reply.

Junior realized this was not going the way he expected. Accustomed to taking charge of his dates, he recognized this one seemed to be slipping away. "Just the Becks, then."

"How long is the course?" she asked.

"Well, it doesn't have a rigid time frame. I mean, as long as you complete the required book stuff within three years. If you don't finish, they—the PGA that is—make you go back in line to the beginning."

"How far along are you?"

He hesitated and felt the nape of his neck grow warm. Junior picked up the fresh beer and sipped, gazing at her over the top of the mug. Ginger had not taken her eyes off him. Her penetrating stare was that of a teacher waiting for a pupil to answer her question.

"Not very," Junior said. This time his ears warmed.

"Oh? So I guess you only just started?"

Junior's first impulse was to lie, say he began this year. At any other time, lies would have tumbled out like an overturned bucket of golf balls. Now, his voice failed him. He was sure Ginger could see through him.

"Two years ago—I started the program two years ago. I'm about a quarter of the way."

Her wrinkled nose did the asking.

"Lazy, I guess," he volunteered, attempting to avert his eyes. Her stare held him. He struggled to remember why he had made this date. The picture of her on the diving board formed in his mind, but the full image would not come.

"That means you have another year to finish three-quarters of the bookwork." Her tone was firm, not scolding. She took the beer from his hand, set it down on the bar, and slid the mug out of his reach. Junior sat still. "A bit of a heroic task. Can you do it?" Again, her eyes held him.

Junior remained quiet, overcome with a strange calmness. He sensed a wall of silence wrapping around him. He could hear nothing except his own thoughts. They became a series of loud sentences in his head. Can I finish the program work within the next year? Of course, I can. If I put in the time. If I get serious. If I knock off the bullshit. I have the ability. I can do it. I'm going to be certified, become a PGA Professional.

Junior heard a soft pop! Looking around startled, he assumed he'd dozed off. He turned to Ginger. She was grinning. With a force of conviction that surprised him, he said, "I know I can."

"I believe you can too. You would be a terrific professional. Tell me something. Isn't your real name Dennis?"

"How did you . . . oh, yeah, the yearbook."

"Right. And the blurb under your yearbook picture said Florida State—golf pro."

"Well, I got a shot at making one of those two goals come true." His voice was firm.

"Where did the name Junior come from?" she asked. "Was Dennis your father's name?"

"Yeah, and when one of the guys on Central's golf team found out, he saddled me with the label. As a joke at first, but soon the whole team picked up on it. Somehow, the name stuck. I became known to everyone as Junior."

"Dennis Boylan would show much classier on a leaderboard than Junior Boylan. Don't you agree?"

He considered the clown who first tagged him with the name. "You know, you're right. I think I've outgrown Junior."

"Dennis, I believe you're on your way." She slipped down from the barstool. "Excuse me, I have to visit the ladies' room," she said and disappeared into the shadows of the Holiday Inn.

* * *

Mike approached Junior the next morning. The lad was alone on Oak Tree's kidney-shaped putting green, a tranquil place where members spent hours practicing in solitude that part of their game requiring severe concentration and studied repetition. He pulled his golf cart alongside the grassy expanse and motioned him over. "Junior, where in the hell is the tee sheet? My guys don't have a clue whose bags we need to load on carts for today's rounds."

Junior looked up from his bent putting position. "I'm sorry, Mike. I forgot to print you a copy. My head's somewhere else this morning." He picked up his putter and walked to the cart.

"Something wrong, boyo?"

The story of last night's date came pouring out while Mike sat listening without interrupting. Junior was short of breath when he finished.

"I mean, it's eerie, Mike. I'm telling you." SMACK! The putter head bounced off the front tire of the cart. "She suddenly vanished into space like she never existed. Disappeared into the ladies' room and never came out. I told myself, well maybe she had enough of me and beat it. That would have been nothing new. It's happened to me a few times, especially when I get sloppy after too many beers. But this time I was stone sober, on my best behavior." SMACK! The putter slammed the tire again. "I tried pulling up her page on the dating website.

She wasn't there. And this morning . . . get this . . . when I called Gold's Gym, they told me they never had a trainer named Ginger Tibsen. I'm baffled, Mike. I don't know what to make of it." He punctuated his frustration with another whack against the tire.

"Well, if you stop and take a breath a minute, I'll see if I can shed some light on the matter. And for goodness' sake, put the damned club away before you hit me."

"Aah, man, I really liked the girl. She got to me, got me wondering about my stupid life here at Oak Tree, got me believing in myself, and all fired up about finishing the PGA course this year. What the hell am I going to do now, huh?"

"You're gonna finish the damn program this year, that's what you're gonna do."

"Yeah, well, I tell you what. I'm going to keep looking until I find her again. And I'll find her, I promise." He raised the putter to slug the tire, and Mike leaped out of the cart with an agility that misrepresented his sixty-five years.

"Hold on, son. Hold on. I don't suppose you'll ever find her."

Junior stopped in mid-take-away. There was a finality in Mike's tone. Lowering the club, he asked, "Why not?"

"Because, boyo, she doesn't exist."

"What the hell you talking about?"

"What I mean is, I don't believe she exists."

"But I spent two hours with her, and she sure as hell existed then."

Mike climbed back into the golf cart. "Get in, son," he said, sounding like a father picking up his child at school. Junior obeyed, and the old man drove toward the practice aqua range.

Several early-riser members were already on the newly mowed range, driving floater balls across the large lake, trying to reach the island green 200 yards out. As clubface and golf ball came together, sharp, metallic pinging sounds rang out in the fresh morning air. Each time a member's club made contact, the snowy-white egrets searching out roots and bugs at the base of the water's edge would take flight, returning moments later farther down the shoreline.

Mike drove to the far side of the practice range, to the end where they conducted lessons, where no one could overhear their conversation. He parked the vehicle and turned toward Junior.

"What I'm gonna tell you is strictly speculation, you understand. You may choose to doubt my explanation, but your experience sounds familiar. Something I've heard many times before." Mike's face was deadpan.

Junior twisted around. "Okay, what the hell's going on?"

"Son, it appears what we have here," and the old man's eyes rolled in their sockets, "is a visit from the Leprechaun of Good Works."

Junior's mouth opened. He remembered hearing the term Leprechaun referred to once during an English lit class in high school, during a discussion of mythical creatures in literature.

"Mike, you been drinking?"

"No, no, I want you to listen to what I'm saying. Leprechauns are an Irish superstition, to be sure. No one has ever disproved their existence. The Leprechaun is a pygmy sprite dressed in green, sometimes living in wine cellars, and often farmhouses. They're supposed to be cobblers crafting beautiful shoes for the fairies." Mike stopped and peered back at Junior. "His other trade is banking," he went on, "and he's also the guardian of their ancient treasures. Legend has it that if you caught one of these creatures, he would lead you to a crock of gold. If you take your eyes off him, he will vanish into the air with the gold."

"Come on, Mike, you're shittin' me now, aren't you?"

"Son, keep in mind this is superstition. Let me ask you something. Did you ever take your eyes off the woman while you were with her?"

Junior mulled over the question. He recalled how difficult it was to turn away from her face when she spoke. "No, I guess I didn't. At least, not for long. Why?"

"Good. Now, I'm not saying you're gonna become a rich man, but by golly, it appears you have benefited mightily from this experience."

"You're telling me Ginger Tibsen was a Leprechaun? Ginger was a beautiful redhead with a body of a goddess. Leprechauns are tiny men dressed in green, aren't they?"

Mike stared out across the lake for several seconds. "Sure'n that's true, lad," he said. "The fact confounds me, too. Nevertheless, you see, Leprechauns work for the fairies, and fairies come in both sexes. Perhaps Ginger was a genuine fairy, a female fairy sent to you to curry favor for the Leprechaun of Good Works. He could have been too busy to make the trip himself." The Irishman paused. "What was she drinking?"

"Only Diet Coke."

"That's it, then. The lore is Leprechauns drink beer, and fairies, only soft drinks."

Junior shook his head. "Jeez, Mike. Either you're bullshittin' me, or I'm the luckiest guy in the world." He stepped out of the cart.

"Where you goin'?"

"I'm going to walk back to the pro shop, Mike, to chew on this alone. My head is pounding. I'm dizzy over it."

"Okay, don't forget my tee sheet and your nine-thirty lesson with Mrs. Baumeister."

Before Mike could start the cart and disappear up the path, Junior leaned in and took him by the shoulder. He squeezed it hard. "Mike, two things I'm sure of."

"What's that, boyo?"

"First, I'm going to hit the books every day after work, and second, no more Junior. I'm using my real name. I'm going with Dennis from now on."

With a twinkled expression, Mike replied, "Perfectly fine with me—Dennis.

LEFTY

The last thing I expected to happen in my section was an attempted murder. I mean, the grandstand is another thing, but in the clubhouse? The damn fool would be facing manslaughter charges today if he pulled it off. Boy! Life is sure full of surprises. Just when you think you got a handle on someone, bingo, he removes the mask.

Phil Myerstein came in with this guest, Jesse Carlton. When I first spotted them, I thought, hey, wait a minute, what's Phil doing with the don? You know, John Gotti, the Mafia boss. Same stocky build, bull-like, not too tall, thick athletic neck, neatly barbered silky-gray hair, handsome in a macho way. Someone you'd expect to find with a blonde Kewpie doll hanging on his arm. I couldn't see his eyes under his dark shades, but I guessed him to be in his middle forties.

For sure, he wasn't wearing a regular off-the-rack job. The suit had to set him back an easy grand. Black sharkskin, double-breasted number, custom-tailored the way it kissed and hugged his frame, topped off with a white shirt and red polka-dot tie. Right outta *Gentlemen's Quarterly.*

Phil Myerstein was the one who has the woman's sportswear company, Casual Fabrics. He also owns Cut Velvet, a three-year-old colt and winner of this year's Flamingo Stakes. Phil called Jesse Carlton a business associate. To tell the truth, I was sorry he didn't turn out to be the Godfather. First of all, he'd been good for at least a twenty-dollar tip, and second, if he was the don, he wouldn't have caused all that trouble.

I studied him because I like studyin' people. Nothing gets by me. I'm careful when I observe, and nobody knows I'm doing it. It's like looking into people's windows. You know, a peeping Tom. Only, they can't arrest me for the peeping I do. My window ain't into someone's bedroom or anything sexy. The closest I ever came to that was the summer years ago when I worked at the beach club as a lifeguard, when the cabana boys used to fetch me from the stand to peek through a hole they made from the chair storage room into the shower stall of the ladies' locker.

No, this kind of peeping is more into the windows of the important money people at the racetrack, watching the way they act with one another. Like the way Nick Carraway did in *The Great Gatsby.* You remember that movie, don't you?

Well, this Carlton guy walked right by me. You'd think he owned the place. He sped down to the front row of boxes and stared out over the railing. Looked like he was trying to figure out where to put the swimming pool. Meantime, I escorted Phil Myerstein to his box a few rows back, and he signaled to Jesse Carlton to come join him.

"How you doin' today, Mr. Myerstein?" I asked. "How'd Cut Velvet come out of the Flamingo?" I could sense he was distracted. He kept looking at the black sharkskin suit coming toward him.

"Not bad, Lefty. Did real fine. He's resting right now, enjoying downtime on the farm."

"Whatcha gonna do, bring him up to run in the Wood Memorial?"

"Haven't decided yet," he said. "Have to talk with his trainer, ask which final Derby prep race he wants to use."

Myerstein's smooth, tanned face appeared grim. A tall man, I'd put him at sixty, sixty-five, manicured fingernails, with slicked back, snow-white hair under his ever-present Panama hat. His suits never varied, single-breasted, light in color—tans, pale blues, and up in Saratoga, white. I never saw him dressed any other way. The contrast with his friend, Carlton, was funny. I almost said something, but I decided he was not in his usual pleasant humor. He had a lot on his mind.

Jesse Carlton flashed by me without as much as a nod. The black suit dropped into one of the chairs in Myerstein's box, and I beat it out of there quick, back to my station.

I'm what's called a White Cap, a fancy name for an usher. Mornings, I work in the backstretch for John Camposino, the trainer, getting up on horses. Been his exercise rider six or seven years now. Early on, I had dreams of riding a Derby winner. A little thing like genetics got in the way. Today, at five-seven, a hundred and thirty-five pounds, I couldn't make the weight if I spent a season in the sweatbox. I keep my hand in by exercising horses. Afternoons, I work the track in the clubhouse section. Between two jobs, I make a decent living, and hey, the tips are all gravy.

That reminds me. I'm known as Lefty around the track. Not that I'm left-handed, but when someone goes to tip me, I always cup my left hand behind my left hip. Then they stuff in their thank-yous, secret-like, since the ones that run the racetrack don't want White Caps taking tips. Can't say why. They just don't. I remember the first time I did the hand-on-the-hip bit. The guy breaks up laughing. Anyhow, I kept doin' it. Now they call me Lefty. The name's really Eddie, and I'm a righty, for sure. Like I told you, life's not always what you think.

I work the entrance to the box seat area, right in front of the Trustees' Room. It's a section of stepped-down rows of open boxes on the second level of the clubhouse overlooking the finish line. Terrific view of the whole track from up there, across the huge, green, landscaped infield and duck ponds to the backstretch. It's a long way across to catch the start of any six-furlong race without binoculars, but you have a perfect angle to see the stretch run from the top of the final turn to the finish line. The mile-and-a-quarter races begin right on the clubhouse turn, giving you a great up-close shot of the horses breaking from the gate. Prime location, it is. Bet on it.

People who come into my section are nice to me. If I can, I treat them good, like trying to improve their seats to a better location. Even let them sit in a box of a prominent horse owner who ain't using it. I hear all the time, "Hey, Lefty, who looks good today?" since, on occasion, I'm privy to inside information.

I don't mean to sound like a namedropper, but plenty of people who come into my section, 'specially on weekends, are famous. Movie stars, Wall Street millionaires, rock stars, baseball players, Broadway show types, TV personalities, and even dress designers. You name it, I get 'em. If I told you who they were, you would be impressed. Guess what, though? They're a sorry lot up close. They're so damned into themselves and all that. And do they love it when they're recognized, always waving and playing kissy-face with people they consider are important too, 'specially the big-money society types. They act as if the track is there only for their personal pleasure. You know what I mean, don't you?

That's why I liked Phil Myerstein. No pretensions. Think about it. Here's a guy with megabucks, a successful clothing business, and nothing short of a Derby contender in Cut

Velvet, yet talks to everybody, treats everyone with the same respect, and is generous when he says thanks. Good people, he is. Comes on weekends with the wife, a real sweetheart, down-to-earth type. Reminds me of Debbie Reynolds.

As a rule, I don't envy many people, wishing I could trade places and that sort of thing. Except Phil Myerstein was my man. He had it all. So when he turned up on a weekday—which was rare unless one of his horses was on the card—with this creep, Jesse Carlton, he surprised me.

We didn't have a large crowd. Not bad for a Monday. The bugler's "Call to Post" drifted up, scaring the hell out of the flock of gulls parked on the railing near the musician.

Thoroughbreds and their lead ponies came prancing through the tunnel, heading out onto the track for the post-parade of the first race. The sun was warm, straight up in the sky, and its bright rays bounced off the jockey's silks. A perfect spring day—still too early for long shadows. The surface condition was fast, dried out from the recent hot spell we were having.

Soon as they loaded the horses in the gate, I caught a glimpse of Jesse Carlton leaving Phil Myerstein's box and go in the trackside door to the Trustees' Room. He ain't supposed to be in there. I guess I should have stopped him, except I didn't want to make a fuss, you know, with him being a guest of Phil's and all that. Figured he wanted to use the men's room there instead of walking around the betting bays to the public restrooms.

The glassed-in wall of the Trustees' Room looked out onto the box area in my section. The plush dining room with dark wood paneling had a maître d' in a tuxedo that runs the room. Very private, very selective. It's the kind of place if they checked your fingernails for dirt before they let you in, you wouldn't be shocked. Cushy, deep carpeting, fancy antique furniture, and white tablecloths and flowers are part of this ritzy atmosphere.

The room is where the track's important big shots eat lunch in quiet air-conditioning. They have their own betting windows to make their two-dollar bets, away from the public's eyes. On most days, you would find a trustee or two dining with their wives. Rich people like Alfred Van Slyke, the chairman of the racetrack, who has nothing more important to worry about than the missing apostrophe in all the men's room signs. Honest! Turned the track upside down one day last year when he found a couple of signs that way.

It gets upper management and their guests, a handful of wealthier horse owners, a couple of celebs, and maybe a heavy hitter or two like Big Joey. It always makes me smile when I look at them standing in line at the buffet together, eyeing each other, trying to appear as though they belong. Oh, yeah, they also let in trainers who have a horse running in the feature race—a feeble nod toward liberalism. I heard a turf writer say that once. For sure, nothing but a snob atmosphere with lots of blond, flat-chested women with skinny legs, talking without unclenching their teeth.

I waited for the posting of prices for the first race. My attention was fixed on the infield tote board, so I didn't notice Jesse Carlton when he returned to Myerstein's box. The winner of the first race was the morning line favorite going off at two-to-one. No question, everyone in the Trustees' Room— except Big Joey, of course—had a bet on it. They love two-to-one shots in there. The term for it is chalk. They win and they think they know something about handicapping.

"I'm gonna grab a dog and soda," I told my relief man when he arrived before the third race. "You want anything?"

"Nah, I ate already," he said. "Take your time. I need to check out this race. Benny, the Clocker, he's been touting the workouts of the three-horse all week. I gotta see if he's just blowing smoke like he usually does."

The big frame of Gotti's double came close to knocking me over as he sped by, disappearing through the Trustees' Room door for a second time in less than an hour. My relief man spotted him too. He reacted but backed off when I pointed to Phil Myerstein, who was standing up in his box, his eyes tracking Jesse Carlton's every step.

This time I trailed Carlton into the room and watched as he threaded his way between tables. He whizzed by the buffet along the back wall with no one noticing, turned left after the two betting windows, and disappeared down a short corridor to a small, private sitting room with a telephone, a courtesy for guests who needed to keep in contact with the outside world.

I exited the room by the front entrance, stepping into the clubhouse interior. As soon as I arrived at the hot dog stand on the other side of the wall separating the clubhouse and grandstand, a familiar voice greeted me.

"Hey, Eddie, how ya doin'?"

Danny Tucker was one of the smartest jockey agents in the business, a first-class race handicapper. The jocks he handled always did well. His talent for getting them mounts was legendary. More than that, he could get the ones that ran fast. Right now, he had the contract for Chris Deveron, the Texan jock he found riding quarter horses at a tiny fairground track in El Paso. Deveron was Cut Velvet's jockey and a favorite of Phil Myerstein.

"You old fraud, Danny. When are you gonna give me a shot at getting my money back? And I definitely want more than three a side. Sixteen handicap, my ass!"

Danny laughed, and the sauerkraut-covered hot dog exploded from his mouth. He had hustled me something awful in the last Horseman's Golf Tournament, a twice-a-year outing where everyone lied like rogues about their handicaps. It had become our running gag.

"Anytime, sport. How 'bout tomorrow? You hustle up any invites yet?" he asked—a not-so-subtle reference to my talent for coaxing invitations out of certain regulars that come into my section. These rich guys, they know I golf every Tuesday when the track is closed. Every so often, they try to show off. "Sure, Lefty, you want to play a round at my club? I'll set it up for you." Especially if I tell them it's for me and a couple of jockeys. Hey, I get to play all those fancy private courses without shelling out the heavy dues.

"One more to load," the track announcer blared over the public address system.

"Tomorrow? Yeah. Matter of fact, me and Jorge Ruiz got a one-thirty tee time at Piping Rock, Mike Streep's club."

"Aaannned, they're off!" the announcer's crackling voice broke in. His echoing race call ricocheted throughout the concrete and steel cavern of the Belmont Park grandstand.

"Who?" Danny asked, tilting up his head and cupping his hand to his ear.

"Mike Streep, Red Coat Farms. You know him?" I asked, forced to yell above the noise of the caller.

"Oh, sure. Chris rides for him once in a while."

"Come along. Mike won't care about one more freeloader. I mean, if you don't mind playing with a jock. Jorge is okay. He's a better rider than he is a golfer."

We consumed our foot-longs side-by-side, while I thought about Jesse Carlton. I asked Danny if he was aware of who he was. I figured as Chris Deveron's agent, he would have more of the inside dope about Phil Myerstein's friends than me.

"He's that corporate-raider guy," he said. "He's attempting to do with Phil's company what Carl Icahn did in the mid-eighties with TWA."

"You mean Carlton's trying to take it over, buy Casual Fabrics?"

"Yeah. There was an article in *The Wall Street Journal* about it last week. Apparently, he made a bid for the company and Phil balked. Now, it's become a hostile takeover situation. Phil is the founder, chairman, and majority stockholder, and he wants to keep control for his heirs."

"You sure we're talking about the same guy?"

"Yeah, I'm sure. Why you asking?"

I pointed my hot dog toward the box seats, flicking relish into the air. "He's sitting with Phil Myerstein. Came in as his guest."

"Jesse Carlton?"

"That's the name Phil gave me." I stopped eating and looked at Danny's curious expression. He looked like he just got a whiff of a stall that needed mucking. "Hey, the guy's been wearing out a path between the boxes and the telephone in the Trustees' Room."

"My guess he's talking with his syndicate, trying to negotiate a deal with Myerstein. Finish up. I'm going back with you. This I gotta witness for myself." He was grinning.

The two huddled figures were visible from where I found Danny a seat. They could have been swapping life stories, the way they were yakking. Carlton would occasionally sneak peeks at his watch and up in the direction of the Trustees' Room. I let my relief man go and toured the box section, figuring to schmooze with some of the golf club set and make a few points.

It was almost three o'clock. The fifth-race post-parade had finished. The horses were loading into the gate on the backside for a six-furlong claimer. Carlton rose from his seat, and Myerstein jumped up to block his way. A rough shoulder from the linebacker in the black suit hit Phil in the middle of his chest. The action happened fast. I almost missed it. For sure, the bump went unnoticed. Most of the surrounding people had binocular lenses pressed against their eyes, or they were busy squinting at the starting gate across the wide infield.

As the starter's red flag dropped on the track, Jesse Carlton sprinted toward the Trustees' Room door for his third trip of the day, with Phil Myerstein in pursuit half-a-length behind. My high sign to Danny was unnecessary. He had already spotted the off-track race.

Danny stood, trying to look through the windowed wall of the private dining room. "My guess is Phil is going to get claimed after all," he said as I approached him.

"What? What's going on?" It was as if I had been looking through the wrong end of the binoculars. Everything appeared far away.

Minutes later, both men bolted out the door. Their running order had not changed. Carlton rushed down the steps of the aisle, his momentum driving him beyond their box seats, Myerstein at his heels, shouting in a voice I never heard him use.

Carlton pulled up at the railing after he realized he had gone too far. The speedy Myerstein's forward motion carried him into the stopped Carlton. Phil's tree-like torso rammed into the back of the black suit. He later claimed he tripped. I guess I was the only one, besides Jesse Carlton, naturally, who noticed that little extra shove Phil put on him. He said he was only trying to regain his balance, but the push was enough to boost the corporate raider over the waist-high railing.

Well, I swear this guy, Carlton, must have worked out on the high bar in college because as he went ass-over-teakettle, he locked onto the railing with one hand. Somehow, he hung on until a handicapper sitting nearby grabbed his wrist. I thought, for sure, he was gonna fly with the seagulls swooping around below.

Danny and me were there in seconds to help pull Carlton up and back over. His face was bloodless, and his eyes bulged bigger than half-dollars. Phil Myerstein sat in a chair at the spot he had "tripped," his head in his hands, shook up, confused, and scared. His hair was a mess, and his Panama hat lay at his feet on the concrete step. A pathetic sight. When I looked at him, I sensed only disappointment. I decided he wasn't somebody I wanted to be.

* * *

The next day on the first tee at Piping Rock, I asked Danny if he thought Jesse Carlton would press charges as he had threatened to do when the cops got there.

"Maybe not," he said, waggling his driver over the top of his teed golf ball. "I don't imagine he wants the publicity."

"I can't believe it. Phil almost killed the guy, shoving him over the railing that way. If the handicapper sitting nearby hadn't grabbed him when he did, Phil might be lookin' at a manslaughter rap today. Think about it. If he'd gone over, he coulda landed on the crowd standing on the apron below the boxes and sent a few horseplayers to the hospital."

"Tell you one thing, for certain," Danny said, "Phil's gonna lose Casual Fabrics. I hear Carlton's group acquired enough shares to take control."

"Yeah? Is that right? Damn, what a shame," I said. The words didn't come out sounding as if I meant them. The click of Danny's ball off the face of his driver changed the subject, and I was glad.

CHINATOWN

It was late morning, and Detective First Grade Alfie Ramos tossed aside the Sunday Times when Fran announced she was ready to leave. Before he could grab his iPhone and pocket it, the cellular sounded with his new ringtone, the opening bars to Dave Brubeck's classic, "Take Five." He'd grown tired of the old doorbell sound, and when he discovered the app featuring a significant selection of musical options, he jumped on the one offering his favorite jazz pianist. Alfie pressed the telephone icon on the screen.

"*Hola*, Alfie," the voice said.

Alfie failed to notice the caller ID, but he recognized Fuentes' voice. "*Amigo, qué pasó?*"

"I had drinks with Eduardo last night."

"Yeah, and . . . ?"

"Eduardo said he knew which sex house in Queens the Salazar sleazebags were holding the two Mexican teenagers. I checked it out with our guy on the inside. The info was correct."

Alfie paused. "Yeah, so I'll contact Lieutenant Rogan tomorrow. See if he'll provide us with backup when we go in."

He sent a quick glance at Fran primping in front of the Barcelona mirror over the couch and lowered his voice. "Thanks, Luis. I gotta run. We're on the way out for a Sunday brunch down in Chinatown. Let's talk again in the morning. See how we want to handle the extraction."

"Okay, *amigo*. Enjoy yourselves," Fuentes said and disconnected the call.

"Ready?" Fran asked and walked toward the door.

"Right behind you."

They strolled up the street to Eighth Avenue, and Alfie flagged down the first taxi he spotted barreling north. "13 Doyers Street," he told the driver when they got in.

The cabbie took off and made a left at Forty-ninth, then headed west to Ninth Avenue for the ride downtown. Alfie planned this to be a discovery trip for Fran. Their destination was a classic dim sum restaurant in the heart of New York's Chinatown, one of the many locations in the city Fran had yet to experience. They would spend a lazy Sunday afternoon sipping tea and feasting on a countless assortment of delicacies.

The Chinese dim sum dining concept, meaning "to touch your heart," was composed of a variety of dumplings, steamed dishes, and other goodies served one at a time in small portions. He was certain Fran would love it.

"Who was that?" Fran asked during their taxi ride.

"Who was what?"

"The person on the phone with you before we left."

Suddenly, another taxi cut in front, crossing over to make a right turn at the next intersection. Their cab driver hit his brakes and swerved to the left. "Damn camel jockey," he shouted out his window. The driver looked into the rearview mirror and mumbled an apology from the side of his mouth.

Fran turned to Alfie. "So who was it on the phone?"

"Huh? Oh. Only Luis Fuentes. He called to say he thinks he knows where they're holding those two kidnapped Mexican girls."

Reluctant to discuss his cases with Fran, Alfie tried to make the call sound routine. Fran had a tendency to assume everything he was involved with was a life-or-death matter, which made him careful not to feed her too much information.

The day was cloudless, and the sun felt good despite a slight chill in the air. The taxi moved downtown along Ninth Avenue, maneuvering through the lighter Sunday vehicle traffic. At Twenty-third Street, the driver made a left going east.

The mild weather invited heavier than usual foot traffic. Impatient walkers, who had stepped out into the crosswalk when the light turned green, often trapped slow responding vehicles failing to get through pedestrian-crowded intersections. The blare of the taxi and car horns made no impact on the speed at which those pedestrians moved out of the way.

"So you know now where they are?" she asked, her voice heavy with concern.

"I'm sorry, hon, what did you say?"

Fran repeated the question.

"We're not sure. We need to talk with someone at the local police precinct in Corona."

At Broadway, the driver turned south and found clear sailing until he pulled up at the entrance of the Nom Wah Tea Parlor. The restaurant was the oldest Cantonese dim sum parlor in New York's Chinatown, opening its doors in 1920. They exited the taxi and Alfie remembered the one-block-length of Doyers Street was the notorious location for the grisly Chinese Tong wars in the early twentieth century. He chose not to share that piece of the city's history with Fran.

The street-level restaurant, centered in a series of connected three-story buildings, displayed a multi-colored awning over its entrance. Inside the unpretentious eatery, a Chinese host in a tight-fitting satin dress with slits up to her hips, showed them to a six-top in the middle of the dining room. A colorful pot of Chinese tea shared the center of the table with an arrangement of fresh lilacs in a tall crystal vase. They were alone at the table, but Alfie figured the remaining four chairs would not be vacant for long.

Carts, each filled with specific dim sum selections, wheeled by the tables, paused to allow diners to choose from the offering or wave it off and wait for the next cart. Alfie saw Fran's mystified expression and resisted a laugh.

"Okay, here's how this works. The servers wheel around those carts. Each cart offers a small appetizer-size portion of different dishes, and you pick out whatever looks good to you. They serve the hot ones in a steamer basket. The cart-pusher marks down what you took, then along comes another cart with other goodies, and you make another selection. You do that until you're stuffed. No hurry. It's the Chinese version of brunch, and it goes on all afternoon."

Her face lit with an expression of delight. "Oh, my. Like filling up on hors d'oeuvres. It sounds like great fun."

Over the next hour, along with many cups of tea, Fran consumed a sesame seed puff, two deep-fried vegetable spring rolls, two baked BBQ pork buns, and a dish called chicken feet. Put off by the name, she tried it anyway and loved it. She ended with a shrimp-stuffed eggplant delight.

Alfie stuck with the more traditional delicacies: shrimp noodle rolls, steamed pork spareribs, three shrimp dumplings, a taro croquette, and a custard tart.

At last, filled with a variety of dim sum selections that more than satisfied their appetites, they sat back and sipped Chinese tea. Alfie's gaze landed on a young girl pushing a cart. As she approached, he realized she was bussing tables. His eyes moved with her, watching her flit from one vacated table to another, clearing them of empty dishes. She appeared to be about fourteen or fifteen.

Fran put down her teacup. "What are you staring at, hon?"

"That kid, the one bussing tables. Her youth made me think of the two kidnapped teenagers."

Fran lowered her eyes. "You're going to find them, aren't you?"

"Oh, yeah." He paused and reached across to take Fran's hand into his. "Watching her reminded me of all those missing kids from so many Asian countries. They're kidnapped and shipped over here by human traffickers. Then they're forced to turn out in the sex trade. Or, at the very least, made to slave long hours at menial low-wage jobs. Employers take advantage of their illegal status."

"And they're brought to New York City?"

"Many of them are, not all. A number of them end up in California, Texas, Michigan, and Virginia. Even Tennessee."

The young bus girl rolled her cart by their table. She wore a man's white dress shirt hung over her denim jeans, and she sported a new pair of white Adidas tennis sneakers. Her ebony hair, pulled back in a ponytail, and tied neatly with a lipstick-red ribbon, glistened when she passed under the overhead fluorescent light fixtures. She possessed a clear almond complexion, and bright, intelligent eyes that darted in every direction while she searched for tables to bus. Alfie guessed her to be the daughter of the parlor owner or from a local family working to earn pin money.

"Are they all from Asia and Mexico?" Fran asked.

"Not all. A lot from third-world countries. Many are sold to sex traders by families to survive their poverty."

Fran's eyes widened and her eyebrow shot up. "They do that?"

Alfie released Fran's hand and leaned back in his chair. "Oh, yeah, often in a lot of the poorer countries, they do.

Listen, trafficking underage girls is a common blight around the world. This country has all but ignored the problem for too many years. The mainstream media doesn't even know it exists."

His attention landed again on the young girl. Thinking aloud, he said, "I can't wait for the Feds to come down on Salazar and his organization."

"Who?"

"Never mind," he said, brushing off his unintended reference to the sex trader.

Fran pushed back from the table and folded her arms. "I want to ask you something. Give me an honest answer."

"Shoot."

"Why did you decide to become a policeman—a detective?"

Alfie raised his chin and stared for several seconds. "I got too old for the Boy Scouts."

Fran smiled. "That's not an entirely mindless answer, is it?"

He thought about the question. "No," he finally said. "I guess not."

"You want to help people. Right?"

"A lot of folks need help."

They remained quiet for a moment. Fran finished her tea and Alfie fiddled with the opened fortune cookie on the table. Without warning, he rose from his chair, moved around, and stood behind Fran. She twisted her head to see what he was doing, and with no overture, he planted a kiss on her mouth before she could open it to speak.

Flustered, she said, "What was that for?"

Alfie laughed. "Because I love you. And hey, this was supposed to be a fun afternoon full of delicious edibles, not spent talking about depressing subjects."

"But this was fun, and I enjoyed listening to you."

He pointed to the empty plates on their table. "Yeah, but did you enjoy all these goodies?"

"Oh, you know I did. Look at all I ate."

"Let's go home," he said, signaling the hostess for the check. "See what additional goodies we can find."

"Wonderful. It'll be my dessert. I'm positive I have room."

FRIENDS

Sal caught sight of him through the window from his position at the end of the bar. He could feel his anger bubbling up. If Buddy wasn't his son, he thought, he might let him dangle in the wind, let the wise guys have at him, teach the cocky kid a lesson. Not gonna happen, he acknowledged, because, as the saying goes, blood is thicker than water.

The Tip Toe Inn was an ordinary storefront saloon in an ordinary middle-class neighborhood in Brooklyn. An aroma of stale beer saturated the air, and over the years, the tang had worked its way into the structure's foundation. Flickering fluorescent tubes hummed from the overhead fixtures, casting their filtered light through a pattern of swirling smoke. A lighted red and green Schaefer Beer neon sign hanging over the back of the bar gave the tavern its only flash of color. Several locals in quiet conversation sat on stools along the dark mahogany bar, while the round Irish bartender moved from one end to the other, keeping glasses filled. All it needed to qualify as an authentic throwback to the thirties was sawdust on the floor and a Wurlitzer jukebox spinning out Russ Columbo favorites.

Sal followed Buddy's reluctant step toward the tavern door. It reminded him of a condemned man on his way to the chair, a scene he saw once in an old Cagney movie. Buddy hated coming across the river, back to the borough of his birth. Except for the fact the kid was in a financial jam, Sal figured he wouldn't show his face for months.

Buddy stepped through the entrance, and Sal gestured to him from the bar where he huddled with another neighborhood regular. Barflies, Sal's wife used to call them, even when the reference included her own husband.

"Buddy, I want you to meet a very dear friend," Sal said as his son slipped onto the stool next to him.

The old man always employed these honeyed expressions when introducing Buddy to a casual drinking acquaintance. If Sal knew him for more than two or three weeks, he would say, instead, ". . . a very dear, old friend." During these semi-sober introductions, it was more than likely Sal would forget to include the person's name.

"Dad, I can't stay longer than one drink," Buddy announced, as though his father measured time in ounces.

Buddy ignored the drinking companion's outstretched hand, but when Sal's facial expression intercepted the near-breach of etiquette, Buddy reached around Sal's back for a cursory shake.

The formality completed, Buddy turned to his father and said, "I gotta be in midtown to pick up Annie before five-thirty. We're heading upstate tonight, and I need to beat the rush hour traffic."

Sal's forehead rippled. "Aw, for chrissake, you're always in a hurry! Slow down and smell the roses, will ya."

As if to illustrate his meaning, the old man threw back his head and, in the same motion, poured the contents of a shot glass down his throat. He swallowed in one gulp, and he chased it with a swig of beer. The ball'n beer was Sal's world, the tavern his social club, and the roses he smelled were Four Roses. He could put away a dozen during a day's sitting and slide down from his stool rock sober.

"What the hell you come for if you don't have time for a drink?" Sal said, his face now flushed with anger and Roses.

"I said, I have time—for a drink—but only one."

Sal knew he had stoked his son's guilt, aware that the slow delivery of his words was Buddy's way of controlling his annoyance.

His son's occasional visits had become more infrequent since Sal's split with his wife. Even when Buddy attended college only thirty-five miles away, he rarely saw him, and then it was with an accumulated load of dirty laundry. "Thank God for dirty laundry," his wife remarked once, "or I'm certain we'd never see him."

"I want to be sure you get the story right," Buddy said, "in case you're questioned about it."

"Questioned about what? What the hell ya talkin' about?" The old man's loud voice caused heads to turn.

"Dad, I told you on the phone when I called this morning."

Buddy eyed Sal's drinking companion. The man sat mummy-like, staring at his hands, holding his beer glass, and attempting to appear indifferent to the conversation.

"Look," Buddy said, "can we sit at a table for a few minutes? We can talk there in private?"

The private reference was not lost on the friend. He spun around on his stool, then dropped his hefty frame to the floor and retreated to the men's room. Sal glared at his son, furious at the rude treatment of his companion. Friends were important, and he reasoned Buddy should have learned that by now.

"For God's sake," Buddy continued, "I'm in trouble, and you never listened to a word I said on the phone this morning. I need to talk to you."

"Lenny, give me another setup, will ya," the old man called to the bartender.

Watching Lenny pour the ball'n beer, Sal remained rigid, his gaze fixed straight ahead. The Irishman set the glasses down, and Sal hoisted them with care, one in each hand, and holding them aloft similar to a tightrope walker's ballast, he slid from his stool to the floor.

"Okay, let's go over there," he said, motioning with a nod of his head to the table in the shadowy back corner of the tavern.

Buddy turned to follow Sal and hesitated as though he had forgotten something. Lenny, the impatient bartender, glared at him. "Just a beer," Buddy finally said.

The barman skated the foaming beer glass along the bar to Buddy. He picked it up and walked to his father seated at the table. Beer suds ran down the sides of the glass, dripping on his trouser leg. He sat down in the hard, rock maple captain's chair opposite Sal and placed his back to the bartender and TV.

"Dad, I got a problem," Buddy said, leaning over the sticky tabletop. "I gotta leave the city for a while until I can cobble together some money."

"Where ya goin'? What's the big rush?"

"Lenny!" one of the regulars at the far end of the bar shouted. "Turn *The Wheel* on, will you? It's almost four-thirty."

Lenny stopped soaping beer glasses in the sink, dried his hands on the dirty white apron wrapped around his bulbous belly, and mounted a box behind the bar. On the tips of his toes, he reached for the controls of the TV set above. Sal looked past his son toward the bartender. His eyes smiled as he recalled the hippos in Disney's *Fantasia*, wearing pink tutus and dancing pirouettes. He'd taken Buddy and his younger brother to see that movie when they were tots.

Sal's attention returned and Buddy said, "My difficulty is Rocco. I'm into him for twelve thousand bucks from the Saratoga meet. He wants to get paid. I haven't got it now, and I need to work out something."

"Well, what the hell you talking to me for? I ain't got that kind of dough." The old man raised his voice louder than he meant to.

"Shush, for God's sake. Calm down." Buddy took a furtive look around and realized no one was listening. The tables surrounding them were vacant. The regulars at the bar were into their own sudsy orbits, and now, *The Wheel.*

"Damn! You shoulda stuck with OTB. Sorry I told you about Rocco."

Sick over Buddy's addiction to playing the horses, Sal had tried to discourage him early on, as he wished someone had done with him when, at his son's age, he first became a player. He was reluctant to give him the bookie's number and relented only after hearing Buddy's constant complaints about the creeps at his local OTB parlor.

Buddy loved the idea of betting with a bookie. All he had to do to get a bet down was pick up a phone. He never had to come face-to-face with anyone except the guy who came around collecting receipts once a week, the goon Rocco referred to as his runner.

"You know, fooling around with these guys ain't smart. They can be dangerous. I warned you from the beginning."

"Yeah, but they gave me track odds, and I didn't have to rub elbows with all that OTB lowlife. I started out betting fives and tens, keeping it under control—"

"And the goddamn credit line hooked you. Right?" the old man blurted. "I told you to watch the credit line before you got in too deep. You didn't listen. So what are you gonna do?"

"That's why I need to talk to you. Rocco's runner comes looking for me, he's gonna approach you first. I want to be sure you don't mention the house upstate where I'm going."

"Why up there? You got money stashed, or somethin'?"

"No, I got two weeks' vacation coming. I promised Annie we would spend it at the house. While I'm there, I'll make a few calls, maybe scare up most of the twelve thousand. But I need time, and Rocco's not giving me any more."

Sal took a sip of beer. "How long you owed it?"

"About six weeks."

"Damn, you must be outta your mind. You be lucky all you get off with is knucks and kneecaps. Buddy, you got a big job, make a fat salary, and got a vacation house in the Catskills. I don't understand why you gotta gamble. You had kids, you might think twice about pissin' away your dough on the damn ponies. When you gonna knock it off? Grow up?" Sal had offered his son this lecture before.

Buddy stood, scraping his chair away from the table. "Dad, I gotta go. I promise once I settle this score, I'm tearing up Rocco's number. I didn't intend to dive in so deep. Annie finds out, she'd probably divorce me. I'll call you in a couple of days and tell you how I'm making out."

The two men moved out from the table. Buddy faced his father and rested his palms on the old man's shoulders. In a lowered voice, he said, "Remember, if the goon comes around asking where I am, all you know is I went somewhere on business. Don't give him any idea I'm trying to duck him, or he might take it out on you. I don't want that to happen."

"Gee, thanks, kid. Listen, Buddy, can you pull it off, find the money, I mean?"

"Yeah, I got a grand right now and eight thousand in a bond fund. The only thing is Annie knows about the investment, and that's my dilemma."

"Well, Buddy-boy, it's both your problem now. You better consider letting her in on your little difficulty, because if you don't come up with the dough soon, she's gonna find out about it, anyway. You get my meaning?"

Buddy's eyes studied his shoes.

"And once you square yourself with Rocco, that's it. No more bets. Get smart, Buddy. I love you. I don't wanna see you get hurt."

Sal walked with him toward the tavern door and stopped, grabbing him by the elbow. "Wait, take a minute and meet somebody." He was looking at the friend, back from the men's room and seated at the bar again.

"I don't have time, Dad. Besides, I already met him. You introduced me when I came in."

"No, I didn't . . . I mean, really introduce you." The old man struggled to penetrate his son's understanding. "I want you should meet him again." His steely fingers gripped his son's arm like a ratchet and cranked him back toward the bar. Buddy resisted, but not for long. Sal's expression said it all.

* * *

Sal watched from the curb as Buddy climbed into the car. He leaned through the open passenger window and told him, "Buddy, you goddamn lucky this time. I mean it. If you don't got scratch for brains, you gonna pay attention to what Rocco told you."

"Don't worry, Dad, I heard him. Honest. Why didn't you say who he was when I first came in? Damn, I treated him like shit."

"Let me tell you somethin', Buddy-boy, don't never treat nobody like shit. Understand? That way, it never comes back to haunt you."

"No, I mean, he's actually a nice guy."

"Course he is. What the hell you think? He ain't no ax murderer. He's a bookie. Makes his living that way. He just don't appreciate gettin' stiffed. Nobody does. Only with him, it can be dangerous."

Buddy moved across the seat, reached out, and laid his hand on the old man's gnarled knuckles wrapped over the window edge. "Dad, I'm sorry. I mean it. Thanks a lot."

"Aah, you don't have to—"

"No, I do."

"Well, stay the hell outta trouble and away from the horses, will you?" He straightened up; his lower back ached from his bent-over position.

"Hey, Dad."

Buddy's call brought him back down.

"Dad, I know I don't visit you as often as I should. I was wondering if you'd like to come up to the house and stay with us for a few days during the next two weeks?"

"Hell, Buddy, I ain't got no way of gettin' up there. Another time. Okay?"

"No, no, I'll drive down and pick you up."

"Nah, that's a bother. I don't want you to—"

"No, Dad. Tell you what. I'll pick you up a week from Tuesday, early morning, say around nine. We can drop you off on our way home the following Sunday. Okay?"

"Yeah? I need to bring anything?"

"No," Buddy said, smiling. "Just yourself."

The car disappeared into the late afternoon shadows. Sal gave it a small wave and strolled toward the tavern, enjoying his warm feeling. Entering, he made straight for his stool at the bar, climbed back up, planted his feet on the brass foot rail, and leaned both arms against the bar's mahogany trim.

"Lenny, do it again," he ordered. "Give him another, too." Turning to his friend, he said, "It'll be fine. He'll come up with the dough, no question about it. May set his little nest egg back a few years. No big deal. He'll make it up. I only hope it learns him good. Thanks for the favor, Rocco. He's a good kid Don't worry. He just needed more time."

"Hey, Sal," Rocco said, "what are friends for?"

DEATH BY DINNER

I can't believe it's Jimmy, except there he is at a table on the far side, in front of the frosted picture window. I hold the menu close to my face and peek again over the top, watching as he reaches under the white linen tablecloth to plant his hand on his newest bimbo's knee. He used to do that with me before we got married. Must mean something special to him, like showing who's in charge, or his way of letting you know what he expects later on. Once we married, though, he stopped. He was too busy doing all those bimbos he had on the side.

I sense my anger beginning to fuel my appetite. I've lived with this reaction since early childhood. Of course, my mother's ethnic family tradition of overfeeding their young never helped matters. Both of my brothers, large, beefy figures today, each weighing in at better than 250 pounds, achieved their size with no more incentive than hearing the word, "Eat!"

Be careful, Mazie, I tell myself. This is how stress used to affect you, always with the same results: a pig-out on junk food, ice cream, chocolates, and enormous amounts of between-meal snacking. In high school, these binges would take over my life until I couldn't stand to look in the mirror. I had to go on a crash diet after each one, which was almost impossible at my mother's dinner table. Thank God, I had the two jumbo bookends sitting on either side of me to take up the slack.

I smile, remembering how, between binges and diets, I got myself voted junior prom queen, and in my senior year, homecoming queen. No matter how heavy I got, I still had the prettiest face in my class at Southside High School.

Ah, but ten years of putting up with Jimmy's constant cheating was the worst. Those resulting binges destroyed me. And the bastard had the balls to call me a blimp right in front of the judge granting me the divorce? I wanted to kill him. The judge did too. She was on Weight Watchers, she told me later and asked if I might like to look at some of their literature.

The waiter returns to take my order. "Ma'am, have you decided?"

"No, Chester, I'm trying to decide. I need more time."

"Yes, ma'am."

I scan the inserted list of specials first before moving on to the restaurant's standard bill of fare. I dine here so often, I can almost recite the menu by heart. My home away from home, cozy and family-like, only without the fat bookends.

Damn! What the hell is Jimmy doing in my place? He said he would never come back here after that first time. He hated it, and he knows this restaurant is my favorite. The odds of running into me are high. Damn him! He's just trying to piss me off. Don't pay attention, Mazie. Shut him out of your mind.

Let's see, should I skip the appetizer? Ooh, wow, they've added stuffed Portobello mushrooms to the menu. I love them. Stuffed with sausage, prosciutto, onions, and roasted peppers, topped with fresh mozzarella cheese, baked and served in a rustic tomato sauce. Boy, doesn't that sound good? I should start there.

Do you believe that son-of-a-bitch? He is actually blowing in her ear. I can't stand looking at him. Stop, you fool. Mushrooms, Portobello mushrooms. Yeah. I'll order them, take them to his table, make like I'm about to bend over to kiss him hello, then I'll grab his oversized Roman nose, hold it and cram the mushroom down his throat—sausage, mozzarella, and all until he chokes to death. Enough, Mazie, you're letting him spoil your dinner. Stop looking.

Okay then, I'll order a salad. They're always fantastic. Oh, here's one I never had. Sliced beefsteak tomato, sliced French Roquefort cheese, and fresh white anchovies over wilted baby greens with balsamic vinaigrette dressing. Jimmy hates anchovies, always picking them out of his Caesar salads. I remember how he almost threw up one time at that restaurant in Miami when he accidentally swallowed two of them he'd missed. He gagged and turned blue. I was afraid he was going to check out. Scared the hell out of me. Okay, I'll have the salad and order it with double anchovies, pick them out, go up behind him, and stick them, one by one, into each nostril. That will do him in, for sure. Cut it out, Mazie. Get back to the menu.

What's the soup special? Let's see. Ooh, Chef Michel must be on tonight. They have his wonderful onion soup. Heritage onion soup topped with a toasted crouton and melted Swiss cheese. That might be too much after the stuffed Portobello and salad. Aah, what the hell, how often do they have it on the menu? I'll force myself.

My God, what's that moron doing now? He's stirring his drink with his finger. Is that the worst display of table manners? He's such a classless act. How embarrassed was I that time on the cruise to the Bahamas, sitting at the captain's table? He insisted on drinking his Coors right from the bottle instead of using the stupid glass. It was like he was with his buddies back in some roadhouse. For God's sake, now he's wearing a napkin tucked in over his tie. Did the fool order the lobster? He hates lobster. Use the bib, you jackass. Oh, shit! Who cares? Stop looking.

Anyway, I'm going to have the soup. Heritage onion is Chef Michel's version, made with Swiss cheese instead of Gruyere. The recipe is unusual but also delicious. Yeah, with Swiss cheese, Jimmy. That's why they don't call it French onion, you dope! Couldn't wrap your pea brain around that idea, could you? Gave me such an argument the first time he came here. Boy, would I like to feed it to him now? Get him a large-size bowl and when he bends down to slurp off his spoon, shove his puss into the soup and hold him there until he drowns. Hey, Jimmy, can you smell the Swiss cheese now? I wonder if you can drown someone in a bowl of soup? All right, Mazie, now you're off the deep end. Get a grip and take a breath, will you? Pretend he's not here.

I fold the menu, lay it across my lap, and reach for my Rob Roy. Before ordering dinner, I generally have two drinks, for medicinal reasons, I tell myself. I discovered a while ago about the digestive benefits of Angostura bitters and made the switch from Scotch on the rocks to Rob Roys.

We had been at one of those boring white-tie construction industry dinners Jimmy was always dragging me to. Before dinner, he suggested I try a Manhattan, and I protested. He said it was better, more sophisticated. "I don't like the taste of whiskey," I said. "I like Scotch."

"So, have a Rob Roy," Jimmy argued. "It's the same as a Manhattan only with Scotch." It was then an overweight wife of one of Jimmy's foremen at our table leaned over and told me of the digestive benefits of Angostura bitters. That's all it took to convert me. The first thing I did when the drink arrived was to eat the maraschino cherry. Boy, did Jimmy ever shoot me a face.

Chester, the server, appears. "Have you decided, ma'am," he says, glancing down at the folded menu on my lap.

"Oh, gee, I'm sorry, Chester. I'm taking a breather. However, I narrowed down the starters. Give me a few more minutes, and I'll be all set."

"Yes ma'am, take your time."

I open the menu again and turn to the entrée listing. I scan down the page and read the description of each item slowly. When I arrive at the leg of lamb, taste buds explode on my tongue. New Zealand leg of lamb encrusted with Dijon mustard and chopped pistachios roasted and served with mint pesto sauce. Accompanied by oven-roasted Parmesan potatoes and green beans amandine. I can almost whiff the heady aroma of roasting lamb and the sweet scent of mint sauce floating from the kitchen, except the strong, choking veil of cigar smoke is filling the air and fouling my senses. It drifts across the restaurant from the smoking section. I glance over and spot Jimmy with the largest cigar I ever saw planted right in the middle of his face.

Oh, Jimmy likes his cigars, long, thin panatelas from Mexico, but I don't remember seeing anything the size of the one in his mouth. It looked as if you would need two hands to hold it. Why the hell are they allowing him to smoke a cigar? Most restaurants prohibited cigars, even in the smoking section. Good lord, everyone's looking at him, and he's puffing away, blowing smoke like a chimney. What an inconsiderate jackass! Maybe I'll finish the leg of lamb, go over there, and beat his head in with the bone. I bet no one in the restaurant would care. Probably applaud me.

My second Rob Roy goes down easily while I concentrate on the dessert part of the menu. I need to wash down the leg of lamb with something sweet, I tell myself. I'll order The Devil's Own Sinful Sundae. Vanilla ice cream rolled in toasted coconut, covered in chocolate sauce, and topped with whipped cream. Oh, good heavens, that'll put me in traction, for sure.

I blink my eyes, irritated by the enveloping cigar smoke, and try to visualize how funny Jimmy would look wearing the Sinful Sundae on his head like a hat. Better yet, I'll knock him out with the lamb bone and keep his body covered with vanilla ice cream until he dies from hypothermia. Isn't that poetic? The son-of-a-bitch dying like the cold fish he is. Great. Kind of like a Mafia rubout. His construction crew could appreciate that.

At first, I think my eyes are watering from the smoke. I blot the moisture on my cheek with the heel of my free hand and realize I'm crying. Ah, Mazie, what the hell are you doing? Why even bother? He is so yesterday, and I don't need to go back to my old habits over his shenanigans anymore. Since the divorce, I have not binged. I'm a beautiful 120 pounds, and that's the way I'm going to stay. Chester passes and I raise the menu and wave it at him.

"Ready now?" he says when he arrives at the table.

I set the menu down. "Sorry, Chester, I changed my mind. I'm not staying."

"Ma'am, something wrong?"

"No, nothing's wrong. I decided I don't need to give in anymore."

I retrieve my handbag and sweater from the adjacent chair, lay a twenty-dollar bill on the table, stand up, and gaze back at the puzzled expression of the waiter. "Don't worry, Chester, I'll be back, some other time when the smoke clears."

As I lace my way unobserved through the tables of diners, I feel like this week's lottery winner. I hesitate at the door behind the huge palm dividing my current world from the past and stare back at Jimmy with his newest acquisition. I shake my head and wonder how long that will last. Ah, Mazie, who gives a rat's ass?

CONCERTOPHOBIA

It was with an inexplicable sense of foreboding that Cal waited at the west end of Grand Central Station near the curving marble staircase leading to the mezzanine level. High above the massive terminal, on the majestic arched canopy, a replication of the celestial universe blinked down at him. Out of habit, he turned his gaze upward toward the ceiling, attempting to identify within sixty seconds the lighted constellations of Orion the Hunter, and the winged steed Pegasus. He had played that game with his son Nick often, whenever they entered the terminal to catch a train.

Who could spot the two constellations first? "Ready … set … go."

"There they are," Nick would exclaim, jabbing at the ceiling with his finger. "I see them, I see them." Cal was always a tad slower with his sightings, and the boy delighted in his victories. They stopped playing the game soon after Maggie's death five years ago.

Now, he stood in the familiar arena of their past contests, searching, not for a constellation of stars, but for the face of his son, trying to find him between zigzagging rivers of quick-paced commuters. After spotting him, Cal shifted his focus to the stranger walking at Nick's side. The young man approached Cal with an unsteady step. Cal felt an immediate wave of impending doom. A second unfamiliar teen followed close behind while Nick's prep school roommate, Brad, dragged along, bringing up the rear.

"How ya doin', dude?" the first strange boy slurred as he neared Cal.

The words hung in the air, competing with the blaring public address system, announcements of train departures and track assignments blending like a mélange of discordant orchestras. The youngster stumbled forward with an outstretched hand, his colorless face empty of expression. Cal reached out, more to offer support than as a greeting. Nick made an attempt at an introduction, speaking the boy's name, but his father failed to hear it. The strange teen's eyes sought refuge behind a pair of wireframe glasses. He appeared to Cal as someone not of this world.

A pained look of concern painted Nick's face. The surreal teenage alien continued to pump Cal's hand. When he let go, Cal glared at Nick.

"It's okay," his son said while bobbing his head with exaggerated enthusiasm. "He got sick on the train. He's gonna be fine."

The second unknown companion, a skinny kid with a mouthful of braces, moved in to prop up his pal. They had traveled on the Metro-North Line into Grand Central Station from their boarding school outside New Haven. Their ultimate destination was a Whips 'n' Chains concert at Madison Square Garden.

"How's it goin', dude?" the voice repeated. His eyes never focused. They stared with a vacant gaze, the way a sightless person might.

Cal eyed the boy's unsteady sway with concern. He seemed to be Nick's age, though not as tall as his son's six feet. A red mop of hair the shade of a seasoned tomato covered his head. The color matched the tee shirt under his gray, pencil-striped vest, no doubt a cast-off from one of his father's discarded three-piece suits. His jeans, torn at the knees, completed a picture of a visitor from another planet.

"My friend, you go to the concert in that condition," Cal addressed him in a wary tone, "I'm afraid you're in for a lot of trouble."

The vacuous expression remained. Cal's words failed to get through, and the youngster's comprehension remained muddled in a veil of fog.

The dude's skinny companion grabbed his arm and yanked him away, struggling against inertia to keep him upright. "Hey, man, chill out! Let's go check out the Haagen-Dazs stand." The two teenagers staggered forward. Each stuttered step of their red, black, and white Nikes squeaked on the terminal's smooth marble surface as they drifted toward the information booth in the middle of the crowded concourse.

Nick shuffled from one foot to the other while his father watched in dismay. What in hell was his son doing with these two bozos? Nick trusted people, Cal reminded himself, taking everyone at face value. However, this time he suspected the boy had miscalculated.

He searched for some logic that would justify Nick's alignment with a pair of companions so unlike his son's style. Did peer pressure supersede common sense? Had the two weird kids been smoking pot or sniffing something worse? His son was never into that world, Cal reasoned. He believed he knew the boy, but now clouds of doubt gathered, and it made him edgy.

Nick remained silent, grimacing and inching closer to Brad, a young version of David Letterman who said "gosh" and "sir" a lot. Brad was Nick's closest friend since their first year in prep school and without question, his levelheaded equal. In Cal's mind, that only multiplied the incongruity of the situation by two.

"Nick, for God's sake, how is that clown going to make it through the night?"

"Ah, Dad, don't worry. He'll be fine." He flipped his head in Brad's direction. "We'll take care of him. It'll be okay, honest!"

"Son, don't make me regret getting you these tickets," Cal said. Nick had called last week asking if his father could tap the contact he had at Madison Square Garden for tickets to the concert. Cal's immediate reaction to the band's name, Whips 'n' Chains, sent chills up his spine. He wanted to tell him, no way; however, he could hear Maggie's voice in his head: Damn it, Cal, stop being such a worrywart.

"Hey, that'll be a tough ticket. I'll take a shot and see," he said. As soon as the words were out, he regretted it. Fear washed over him when he flashed back to a frightening incident he read about years ago, the infamous Altamont, California Rolling Stones concert where a Hell's Angel, hired as a security guard, killed a young fan who got out of hand. The image of a packed Madison Square Garden of screaming fans of the Whips 'n' Chains fueled his dread.

Maggie's passing five years ago thrust him into the role of a single parent, giving him sole responsibility for his son. With it came a sea of worries. He lived through those years of turmoil dealing with his survival without his wife. Facing this concert risk with his only child pushed the envelope of worry.

"How many you need?" he asked hoping the event had sold out weeks ago.

"Four."

"Four? You're kidding, aren't you?"

"Besides Brad and me, I need two for a couple of friends at school. We'll pay for them."

"You bet you will," Cal said, "but four. That's expecting an awful lot."

"Well, see what you can do for at least two. I didn't promise the other guys, only that I would try."

"Sounds like a case of teenage foot-in-mouth," Cal had teased.

His connection was reliable. The head of Madison Square Garden security came up with four tickets. Cal recalled the security chief's cautioning words: "I gotta tell you, there's no shortage of headaches at these things. Everything from drug overdoses to alcoholic arguments, pickpockets all over the place, and fights."

Later, when Cal phoned to tell Nick of his ticket success, his mounting concern provoked him to admonish the boy. "Damn it! Don't talk to anyone, and stay together."

"Don't worry, Dad. We will."

Cal hardly expected him to bring along additional trouble in the form of the dude and his friend.

Surrounded by a bustling crowd of commuters, he took Nick to one side. The tickets held tight in his grasp, he wrestled with the temptation of scrapping the deal and writing off the four hundred dollars. "Look, son, I have bad feelings about this. How you getting to the Garden?"

"We'll walk. It's not far," Nick said, as though his father required a geography lesson.

"Hey, I know how far it is. I live here. Remember? I'm worried about you getting there with the geek and his friend." Cal hesitated to ask what drug the geek was on.

"Dad, we'll take care of him. We'll get him there. Trust me, will you?" The eavesdropping Brad nodded in eager agreement.

Despite his angst, Cal realized he had to let go. He didn't want to embarrass Nick in the presence of his best friend. "Okay, here's the tickets." He handed him the four in exchange for a fist of wadded-up bills the boy had collected from the others. "What train you making back?"

"Don't know. Whenever the concert gets out."

"What time is that?" Cal probed.

"Around eleven, eleven-thirty. I guess."

"Fine. Remember what I told you. Don't talk to anyone, don't give anyone a hard time, and mind your own business. After it's over," he added, "come right back here to catch your train. Got that?" Letting go was not coming easy.

Nick climbed the stairs to the mezzanine level at the Vanderbilt Avenue exit and turned to give a final wave to his father. Cal remained in the middle of the crowded concourse feeling alone. Did he do the right thing? The question burned his conscience. If Maggie were present, she would have told him to relax, take a deep breath, and cut the boy some slack. She enjoyed a much higher tolerance for matters requiring blind faith.

Cal tried to console himself, knowing he and his wife worked hard to instill the proper values in their son, from the moment Nick could grasp words and concepts. Be your own person, make your own decisions, and above all, take responsibility for them.

He reflected on his son's first sixteen years when peer pressure served as Cal's constant enemy, and he took great pleasure in knowing Nick's moral character had been praiseworthy, particularly during the last five years after breast cancer took Maggie. Cal figured if Nick wasn't guilty of any questionable social behavior by this time—other than the green, plastic salamander dangling from his left earlobe— the mold had been set. At least he thought so until his son's school chum addressed him as "dude" in the middle of Grand Central Station.

* * *

After showering, Cal stretched out on the sofa in the living room and clicked the TV remote to watch the late news. The commentator on the eleven o'clock report was in the middle of a story that caught his attention. ". . . . a teenager from the New Haven, Connecticut area was injured tonight in the melee during the Whips 'n' Chains concert at Madison Square Garden. They took him to Beekman Downtown Hospital with a broken arm and suffering from lacerations and bruises around the face. Three others involved suffered minor injuries. They were treated and released. The fight broke out when one of the young fans, allegedly high on an undetermined substance..."

Skipping the rest of the report, Cal peeled off his pajamas and dressed. What a fool, he agonized. Why, in God's name, did I give him those tickets? The painful twitch of guilt would make sleep impossible until he knew his son was safe.

He would walk the half-mile to the station. At this late hour, cabs were scarce. No point wasting time searching for one. He slipped on his jacket and searched for his keys. "Where the hell did I put them?" he mumbled. A moment later, he sensed Maggie saying, Look on top of the bureau. He did and found them there, swept them up, bolted out the door of the apartment, and rode the elevator down to the building's lobby.

After a combination of fast walking and jogging six blocks and two avenues, he arrived at the terminal out of breath. Despite the night's coolness, perspiration collected on his forehead.

The large, busy schedule board above the row of ticket windows rolled over departure and arrival information. Nick's train, scheduled to depart at eleven forty-five, gave him twenty minutes to kill. He planted himself in front of Gate 21 and waited and worried.

The concourse bustled with activity despite the late hour; mostly young people. Then he remembered. The crowd represented the many that attended the concert and were now heading home. Whips fans traveling to Connecticut, Westchester, and remote upstate areas rushed to board their trains with memories of the performance fresh in their minds.

Nick had reminded him last week that the legion of devoted fans attending a Whips 'n' Chains concert always wore it as a badge of honor. "Hey, man," he mimicked on the phone, "did you catch the Whips' last concert at the Garden? No? You missed them, man? Let me tell you, they killed!" To say you attended a concert, he informed his father, was worth more than the price of admission. Cal didn't argue, making the leap of faith for fear that his sixteen-year-old Whips follower would cite him for being too old to understand.

Cal scanned the scattering faces and failed to notice Nick and Brad approaching from the opposite direction. The boy's voice broke his concentration.

"Dad? What are you doing here?"

Before replying, Cal ran his eyes over him searching for bandages, Band-Aids, or any other sign of skirmish damage. "Nick, you alright?" he said, noticing the other two companions were nowhere in sight.

"Yeah, of course. I didn't know you planned to meet me after the concert."

"On the news tonight . . . the story about the riot at the Garden. The reporter said it involved kids from Connecticut . . . that one of them suffered injuries. I got worried."

Brad interrupted. "Riot, sir? Gosh, what riot? We never saw anything, at least not in our section."

Everything about them looked normal—iPod earbuds dangling around their necks, and the young Letterman look-alike clutching an opened bag of M&M's. Cal exhaled with relief. He fought the urge to reach out and hug his son. Instead, he asked, "Where's the dude and his friend?"

The question sat unanswered for a moment while both teens stared at each other. Cal pressed, "Are they all right?"

Brad finally answered. "Gosh, sir, Hobbie flipped out during the concert. The security people took the four of us down to the nurse's station."

"Hobbie's your dude friend, I assume?" Hobart, Cal thought. A family name. Why else would anyone name a kid that?

"Yes, sir."

Nick jumped in. "After they found out what he took on the train, they sent him to a hospital in Manhattan."

"Beekman Downtown Hospital?"

"That's the one. Anyway, Charlie stayed with him. Brad and me, they told us to go back to our seats."

"And . . .?"

"They called Hobbie's parents in Westchester to come to pick them up."

"My God, what did he take?"

"He told them it was LSD," Nick answered.

"LSD? Are you serious? I haven't heard of anyone using LSD since they put Timothy Leary away. I'm shocked."

"Who's Timothy Leary?" Brad asked.

"Never mind. Where the hell does a kid lay his hands on that kind of drug these days?"

Nick, smiling at his father's naiveté, replied, "Dad, you can get any drug you want today, as long as you have the money."

Cal stared into the boy's face. "Yeah, yeah, I guess I knew that." At once, the unspoken part of Nick's response hit him like a punch in the gut. His son was from privileged circumstances, money aplenty, yet he had remained strong. The mold set. He and Maggie did a good job.

The four-sided clock over the information booth approached eleven-forty-five. "Hey, you guys better get a move on."

Brad reached out and shook Cal's hand. "Gosh, sir. Thanks for getting us the tickets."

"You're more than welcome, Brad."

Cal opened his arms and wrapped them around his son's back, pulling him in.

"Yeah, Dad. Thanks."

"I'm sure glad you guys are all right."

"I'm sorry. If I had known about Hobbie's—"

"Never mind. You're both okay and that's what counts. Off you go or you'll miss the train."

The two teenagers bounded through the gate and down the platform. Cal opted not to hang around. In the past, when Nick returned to New Haven after a weekend with him in the city, he always waited until the train pulled out. No longer. He could stop being a worrywart.

Cal traversed the concourse, passed the circular information booth, and headed toward the Forty-Second Street exit. He paused in front of the long line of empty ticket windows and glanced up at the vaulted blue ceiling. Spotting Pegasus blinking down at him, he smiled.

AND . . . THEY'RE OFF

The room was graveyard silent until the cue ball clipped the eight ball, sending it caroming off the side of the three tightly packed solid-colored balls, and spinning dizzily toward one of the corner pockets. The game-ending scratch thudded against the dark leather webbing and disappeared below the table. Grady Manning, a boyish-appearing twenty-eight-year-old exercise rider, watched the last of his one hundred and forty-five-dollar stake chase the black eight ball into the hole like Alice's rabbit. His elbows remained pinned to the padded rail of the pool table for several seconds; the muscles of his arms flexed with tension. With slow deliberation, he stood erect and slammed the rubberized butt-end of the cue stick to the floor.

A chortling sound came from the back of the winner's throat as Rudy Garcia rolled his cue stick between the palms of his hands like a Boy Scout trying to ignite a campfire. The pint-size Panamanian liked to punctuate his victories that way, his trademark gesture before racking the balls for another game. Grady had seen it all too often in recent weeks. Damn! Why did I give in to Rudy's challenge? Shoulda told him to take a hike. Grady stood riveted, not speaking, rocking in his scruffy riding boots, a wave of anger washing over him, fingers tightening around his cue stick. What a God-damn bummer. Rent money down the drain, and there goes my shot at getting in on a hefty score too.

The Aqueduct Racetrack recreation hall, empty except for Grady and Rudy, would soon fill with backstretch workers once they completed morning chores. Grady, normally unflappable with annoying situations he knew were beyond his control, rolled his head, trying to stretch the pain gripping the left side of his neck. He took in the room's emptiness, thankful no one else had witnessed his pool-playing humiliation.

"That makes a hundred forty-five bucks, *amigo*," Rudy said.

"I know, yeah, I know. Damn! You don't need to remind me."

"You wanna go another?"

"I'm busted. No more today." Grady walked to the wall rack, replaced his cue, and pushed his hand into his jeans pocket. It remained there for a moment until he turned toward Rudy. "I guess you want to get paid now?"

"Hell, ya think? I ain't running a charity, you know."

"Okay. I was just asking. Don't get tight-ass on me."

Grady used the surface of the pool table to smooth out the wadded pile of money he took from his jeans. In a slow, methodical fashion, he counted out one hundred and forty-five in twenties, tens, and ones. He reached out to Rudy with the handful of bills and pulled back at the last second.

"It's my landlady. She's busting my balls. I'm two weeks late as it is." Grady tried to keep his voice from sounding self-pitying.

"Sorry about that, *amigo*. You shoulda thought about it before we broke the pack. Besides, I'm the one outta work. My trainer took his string of horses to Florida for the season.

I need the dough now. 'Least you have a job. You make decent money. Am I right? Tips too. You doin' better as a clubhouse usher than an exercise rider. Maybe it's a good thing you lost your mounts."

"Hey man, don't go there." Grady rolled his eyes and turned away, certain the wiry groom wasn't going to cut him loose.

"Well, *amigo*, blowing your paycheck bettin' the horses you work is your business. Ya know? I mean, you gotta admit, passing inside dope on them to your buddies ain't smart. Pissed off your trainers. Right?"

Grady's neck muscle tightened again. A wave of desperation came over him. He considered retrieving his cue stick and breaking it across Rudy's hard head. That would give him great pleasure. Instead, he turned to his antagonist while gripping the stack of currency in one hand and thrusting out the other hand as if trying to stop time and fate in their tracks. "Hold it a minute, Rudy. Listen to me." His voice lowered to create an aura of confidentiality. "I got a shot at making some real dough for both of us," Grady said.

His eyes scanned the game room, feigning a search for eavesdroppers before continuing. The emptiness of the backstretch workers' recreation hall echoed back. The ploy worked. Grady had captured Rudy's attention.

"A guaranteed sure thing, but I gotta have the cash to get in on the deal." He raised the wad of money in his hand and flapped it around like a flag. "I promise you, man, this is small potatoes compared to what we can make if you let it ride for a little while. You interested?"

Rudy's gaze fixed on Grady's hand. "Come on, *chico*, you jerkin' me around to get outta paying? Because if you are, I ain't—"

"No, man, I'm not playing games," he said, his voice now noticeably strained. The hands on the clock above the doorway sat close to the time when backstretch workers would soon drift in and end their privacy. Grady's head swiveled side-to-side, taking in the surrounding area. "I got this chance, man, a chance to make some real dough. A legit, no-risk deal up at this Massachusetts track." He gestured toward the green felt of the pool table. "If I settle with you now, I won't have enough cash to get in on it. Maybe you want to go in with me? Score a pile of money. Yes?"

"What's it gonna cost? And who else is involved?"

Despite Rudy's suspicions, Grady knew he'd piqued his interest. He needed to involve him now. If he couldn't hook him before paying off, he would lose him. Rudy was a spontaneous gambler, not a cerebral one. You never wanted to give him too much time to think.

"Three bills, that's all. The deal's total's gonna cost three grand. The trainer told me I could have ten percent. Whaddaya say?"

"Who told you? Who's the trainer?"

"You in or not? I'm not saying who's involved until you're in. If it was your deal, you wouldn't want me dropping the trainer's name all over the place, would you?" Grady hoped the Panamanian would buy into his pissed-off response as further proof of the deal's legitimacy.

The screen door banged open. Grady recognized a hot walker and two grooms entering the foyer area, heading for the rack of cues and the second pool table. He ignored them, waiting for Rudy to reply.

"Okay, *amigo*, I'm in. Now, who's the trainer, and what's the deal?"

"Let's go outside, take a walk over to the backstretch kitchen. I'll buy you a coffee and explain," Grady said.

* * *

The backstretch kitchen was alive with activity. Loud, hurried conversations filled the eatery in both English and Spanish. The smell of burnt toast and leftover chili permeated the air. Grooms and hot walkers occupied the linoleum-top tables, gulping black coffee and wolfing down buttered rolls between wild hand gestures. After working their mounts under the scrutiny of their trainers, exercise riders would soon show up to add to the noise level.

Rudy sat across from Grady at a table in one corner of the kitchen blowing into his hot coffee mug. He looked up. "So how do you figure in this? Why is Joey Brandt willin' to cut you in on his action?"

"I used to work for him before he got suspended up in Saratoga that time for using Bute on the filly, Skip Home."

"Yeah, he knows you. I get it. But why he cuts you in?"

It was the same question Grady asked Brandt when the trainer approached him a week ago with his proposition. The flattering answer Brandt gave him smelled of pure horseshit. The trainer had asked him if he wasn't the one hooked up with his assistant trainer, Kathy Williams. Yeah, of course, Grady had replied. Brandt told him he respected her choice of boyfriends, and he took it as a sign of confidence in his trustworthiness. For certain, the trainer was yanking his chain. Grady signed on despite his initial hesitation, convinced if the deal did turn out to be legit, it would be easy money. And after all, how could he walk away from a shot at a big score?

Rudy opened his mouth about to follow up with another question, but Grady cut him off. "We had a bunch of first-class stakes horses back then, and I got up on most of them. Nobody around worked a horse the way I could, and Brandt knew it. He trusted me."

"Yeah, you were a good rider, *amigo*. Heard you tell that story a couple of times, 'bout why you didn't make it as a jock 'cause of your weight and all that. It's not why he cuts you in, right?"

"No, man. He needs a cover. Someone to get the bet down for him at the track."

Rudy stared back through empty eyes.

Grady could feel his throat closing. He waited for ten seconds, inhaled audibly, and then continued. "He can't do it himself since they might recognize him and blow the whole deal. Massachusetts Downs is a small-time track, but you never know. Horses that ship from other tracks can raise red flags with smart handicappers."

"Oh, you mean if they knew he was running a horse in a claiming race, he might lose him? Somebody might claim him. Right?"

Grady spread his hands and ironed them along his thighs. Rudy's mental slowness irritated him. He wanted to tell him that, but not now. "Well, yeah, that too, but Brandt's not worried about High Hopes getting claimed. He's raced the colt lightly, and no one has any idea how good he is. Brandt has kept his recent bullet workouts under wraps."

"He win yet?" Rudy asked.

"No. Has no better than a third. Dropped him down in class once. Now Brandt's ready to move him up again. He wants to nail down this score first. Kathy Williams is his assistant trainer, and she'll be handling the horse at the race. He won't be up there."

"So, what's he needin' you for if he's got your girlfriend taking care of business?"

"I already told you, to make the bet for him. They could recognize her at a window and blow the whole deal. If the wise guys spot he has a shipper running, they could end up betting down the odds and ruin everything . . . a shot at making a bundle. You get it now?" Grady put a knuckle between his teeth and bit down. Rudy failed to notice.

* * *

The four-hour drive up through Connecticut and Massachusetts turned into a New England postcard experience. Once they left the interstate, driving became a series of "oohs" and "Look at that!" The fall colors were ablaze throughout the panorama of small towns and hamlets. They pulled to the entrance of the Country Inn of Williamstown at dusk.

Grady waited in the lobby while Kathy went to the desk to check in. Any other time, she would have made the trip in the van with the horse the morning of the race, sandwiched between the driver and groom. This time Joey Brandt suggested she go up the night before with Grady. In addition to paying Grady's expenses, Brandt also threw in a night for both at one of New England's most beautiful country inns. As his assistant trainer, Kathy would always have a per diem allowance for travel to out-of-state tracks, but nothing close to covering what the Country Inn of Williamstown would cost. Grady smiled. *Joey Brandt's got class. And why not? He's in for a big payday.*

He glanced around at the hotel's luxury and wondered if sex with Kathy tonight in this ritzy hotel would be any different from when they did it in her small, one-bedroom apartment in Queens. The fantasy vanished when he remembered she needed to be up before first light and at the track to meet the van bringing up High Hopes.

After dining at the inn's four-star restaurant, Grady led Kathy to a table in the cocktail lounge at the other end of the lobby. It was a warm, wood-paneled room with four-top tables and a large stone fireplace as its centerpiece. Flames from well-dried logs crackled over muted conversations and produced a perceptible haze floating above the heads of the guests.

Grady ordered Irish coffee for both. He wanted to remind the departing server that the fireplace flue needed cleaning, but fearing he'd sound like a wiseass, he swallowed the words.

"Dinner was great," Kathy said. "By the way, you didn't say anything to Rudy about where we were staying, did you?" She had been staring at the bar, at two men sitting on stools with their backs to them.

"Yeah, I had to. He would have insisted on coming if he believed we were booked into a Motel 6. He said he wanted to keep an eye on his money, but he wouldn't go for a room at this place. Thank God for that."

Kathy continued to stare.

"What are you looking at?" Grady turned his head to check and muttered in a low voice, "Oh, shit!"

* * *

The late afternoon sun bathed the track, assuring a dry surface for the race. Grady stood in line at one of the grandstand's betting windows. He figured he would be less likely to run into the two syndicate handicappers if he avoided the clubhouse. High Hopes, no longer at the morning-line odds of thirty-to-one, was still a long shot. He noticed the colt had attracted some of the local's money, but even small-town tracks had their share of savvy bettors. He hoped that didn't include the two syndicate guys from last night, but he wouldn't rule them out.

Brandt planned to have Grady place the bet during the last few minutes before post time. "That way," he told him, "your betting action will be too late for anyone to get wise. A three-grand bet was major at small tracks like Massachusetts Downs. It was certain to attract the attention of a smart handicapper watching the odds board."

Third in line, Grady could view the TV monitor over the betting window displaying the latest odds for the eighth race. The digital clock showed four minutes to post. The locals had bet down the odds on High Hopes. He was now twenty-to-one. Grady surveyed the windows to his left and right. None of the lines was shorter. He felt his heartbeat quicken. The horses would soon be loading at the gate. Damn! I'll never be able to face Brandt if I get shut out. And Rudy, he'd go bonkers.

The handicapper at the window finished his transaction and turned to leave. The next man in line stepped up and proclaimed with the confidence of Donald Trump, "Give me five bucks across the board on Bright Star, the seven-horse." Fifteen dollars changed hands, and the tote machine spit out a pari-mutuel ticket on the two-to-one favorite.

Grady moved to the window. "Three thousand to win on the four-horse," he said in a whispered voice. He shoved thirty fanned-out one-hundred-dollar bills through the small opening of the glass enclosure. The clerk looked up from the tote machine and stared out. Grady repeated the wager, louder this time. "Three thousand to win on High Hopes, the four-horse. Hurry, damn it!"

The pari-mutuel clerk took the money and entered the bet. The machine produced a whirring sound as it processed his ticket. When the machine popped it out, Grady exhaled. He reached in before the clerk had it in his hand. A glance up at the TV monitor revealed he'd made it with one minute to go. But he also saw that the odds on High Hopes had changed. "Son-of a bitch," he mouthed as he stepped away from the window. The two syndicate guys had waited until the last minute before placing their bet. They had punched down the odds on the horse to six-to-one. The race's long shot was now a chestnut shipper from Maryland called Spoiled Rotten. This was not what Grady expected. Seconds later the bell sounded, and the betting windows closed.

"Aaannnd . . . they're off! The words from the public address system echoed off the concrete ceiling of the grandstand as the eight Thoroughbreds broke from the starting gate.

Grady hurried across the broad apron of grass separating the grandstand seats from the trackside rail. He heard the track announcer's call and wondered where Kathy went to watch the race.

The eight Thoroughbreds, bunched tight, sprinted down the backside. The race at six furlongs meant the horses would cover the quarter of a mile in little more than a minute. Grady eyed the odds on the infield tote board. He noticed Spoiled Rotten, the other shipper, got off at twenty-to-one while the bettors made High Hopes their second choice at six-to-one. The favorite in the race was Bright Star, a Massachusetts-bred roan colt. The sounds of his cheering section in the grandstand made it obvious he'd received most of the locals' action.

Grady stared at the tote board displaying the running order in lighted numbers until he spotted the horses coming into the turn at the top of the stretch. He focused his binoculars up the track. The horses' positions had remained the same since the eight contestants leaped out of the gate. Bright Star led by a slight margin with High Hopes and Spoiled Rotten nestled in close behind. A gap of two lengths separated them from the remaining five horses. None of the trailing horses appeared to have enough left to become a threat in the stretch. The three front-runners took the turn and straightened for their sprint to the wire. Bright Star was on the inside losing ground rapidly. High Hopes, out from the rail in the number two path with his nose in front of Spoiled Rotten, failed to hold it. The long shot, Spoiled Rotten, as if the recipient of a dramatic burst of energy from a divine source, pulled away at the eighth pole and crossed the wire a full two lengths ahead of High Hopes and three lengths ahead of Bright Star. Grady couldn't help noticing Spoiled Rotten's jockey never touched the horse with his whip.

* * *

Grady knocked on the frame of the screen door. Dried paint flaked under his knuckles.

"Yeah, come in," the voice from inside summoned. "Be with you in a minute."

Grady entered the small windowless office of Joey Brandt, a twelve-by-twelve room at the far end of Aqueduct's barn number 24. The place was familiar. He had been inside the office many times over the two-year period he exercised horses for the trainer.

Seated at his desk with his iPhone to his ear, Brandt spoke in a loud voice as though he had a bad connection. A modern swivel chair carried his lanky frame from side to side as he conversed. With his free hand, he motioned Grady toward the chair at the side of the desk.

Grady's eyes worked around the room as he tried to appear casual, pretending he wasn't listening to Brandt's conversation. He smiled, remembering how the appointments in Brandt's workplace differed from many of the more successful trainers around the track. Nothing had changed since his last visit: the worn-out, over-stuffed leather sofa against one wall, often utilized as Brandt's snoozing place, the antique oak cabinet to the left of it that held a supply of saddlecloths, caps, goggles, shadow rolls, and several pairs of blinkers. A dozen framed winner-circle photos decorated the length of one wall. They showed Joey Brandt, strands of his long sandy-blond windblown hair covering his brow, standing next to the victorious Thoroughbreds, and smiling warmly.

"Yeah, a matter of fact, he just walked in," Brandt spoke into the phone. "No, he hasn't any notion. . . . That was the idea, wasn't it? . . . Yeah, well right. I'm going to explain everything now, bring him up to speed. . . . Yes, of course, we made the deal. . . . Okay, Buddy, we'll talk later. Bye." Brandt fiddled with the power-off button while Grady waited. "That was Brad Phillips down in Pimlico," he said. "He's the trainer of Spoiled Rotten."

A loud bell went off in Grady's head. He swallowed hard and looked at Brandt. A smirk had formed on the trainer's face like a sunrise.

"The race," Grady said, "it was a boat race, right?" He wasn't certain, but the words spilled out before he could stop them.

"Not at all. Spoiled Rotten was legitimately the best horse in the race."

Grady shook his head as if to jostle the fog closing in on his mind. "Then why did you run High Hopes and back him as though he was a sure thing? I don't understand."

"To divert attention from Spoiled Rotten. Make it appear to the syndicate boys like we planned to slip High Hopes into a walkover and cash in big time." Brandt's smile broadened. "Minutes after saddling the horse in the paddock and giving a leg up to his jock, Kathy sprinted up to the clubhouse to lay down another three grand just before the closing bell. This time on Spoiled Rotten while his odds were still twenty-to-one. Grady, you took part in the cover-up. High Hopes was the stalking horse, and you helped paint the picture real."

The cloud lifted slowly, but Grady needed more answers. "How did the two high rollers find out? How'd they come to be staying at the same hotel as Kathy and me?"

"You're not going to believe this." Brandt let a few beats go by before continuing. "It was Rudy Garcia. I tried to leak it to the syndicate boys, you know, about shipping High Hopes to the Massachusetts track. I knew they'd suspect something was up and want to get in on the action. But Rudy got there first."

"Why? I don't understand. Why would Rudy risk blowing the deal? He had a stake in it."

"He wanted a bigger payoff. So he offered to tell the boys about the setup for a piece of their action. When they doubted him, he used the hotel info as proof he wasn't lying. They bought it and went down big on High Hopes. Got a phone call from them last night when they got back from Massachusetts. Said they hated getting beat but admired the scheme. Yeah, sure. Not on your life. They were pissed. I gotta believe your boy Rudy is in deep shit."

The young exercise rider sat frozen in the chair, trying to absorb the information. His head pounded like the surface of a racetrack during a stretch run. He felt used, but most of all, he felt dumb. Why did he buy into Brandt's generous offer to cut him in, provide the all-expense trip, the four-star hotel? And Kathy? She never breathed a word of it on the drive home. In on it from the get-go, she was. His temples pulsed.

"Grady, I can guess what's goin' through your head," Brandt said. "I don't mean to sound preachy, but this business is tough and full of risks. Soon as you believe you're the smart one, someone comes along and outsmarts you. Honest, man, we couldn't have pulled it off without you. Buddy and me needed to keep you in the dark about the real bet. It was the only way to protect the setup, to make it believable. You played your role perfectly, and you know how easy plans can go sour with these kinds of things."

Grady's mind flashed to his tarnished reputation and why he could no longer get mounts. He winced. Yet Joey Brandt had trusted him to deliver even though the part he played wasn't what he thought it was.

He got to his feet, resigned to his misfortune, and said, "Okay, Joey. At least I make a good shill. And what the hell, I got to stay at a famous inn."

The trainer rose from his chair, his hips leaning into the desk. "Grady, the bet paid off a cool sixty-thousand. I promised you ten percent, didn't I? Your money was on the wrong horse, although that wasn't your fault."

"You mean I still get my payday? You're not playing with me, are you, Joey?"

"Not at all, pal." Brandt reached into the right-hand drawer and pulled out a large envelope and held it out to Grady. "This is yours. You earned it. Of course, there's the matter of your greedy Panamanian friend, but then I leave that to you. Now you can square up what you owe Rudy. To be honest, I don't see he deserves anything more than getting back his half of your original three-hundred-dollar investment on High Hopes."

Grady waved the envelope. "I guess I'll have to spring for dinner tonight," he said with a smile. "Kathy knows, doesn't she?"

"You better take her someplace really nice, or she might not have you back as the exercise rider on High Hopes."

"You mean—"

"That's right. You can start getting up on him in the morning. By the way, just so you know, the horse has real potential to be a stakes winner. He was a tad too green to take on the likes of Spoiled Rotten, but he needed the race anyway."

Grady's face lit up.

"Before you bust a gut," Brandt said, "let me caution you not to talk about this to anyone. The wise guys are gonna think you knew about the bet on Spoiled Rotten. They saw you in the hotel. I wouldn't give them any reason to get on your case. Like I said, they're pissed as hell and can get rough if you do anything to embarrass them."

"Don't worry. I'm not lookin' to commit suicide," Grady said as he headed out the door.

MIXED BLESSINGS

The old man shuffled into the clean, well-lighted restaurant at the corner of his street. As always, he took a seat at a table by the window. He liked to gaze at his neighbors as they passed by to shop at the local supermarket next door. The restaurant was quiet with only a few lingering customers at the end of the lunch hour.

The sound of children at his back surprised him.

"No, let me do it," a boy's voice demanded.

The old man turned and saw a young girl holding up a crayon out of the reach of a little boy.

"Okay. I get to do the next one," the girl said before she relinquished the crayon.

"I'll have the special," the old man told the waitress when she arrived at his table. "Only put the salad dressing on the side, will you, Deb? I'm trying to lose a little weight. You know how that goes."

She scribbled on her pad and raised her head. "You okay here, Al?" she asked, nodding toward the table behind him. "There's a two-seater over by the door if you prefer."

Debbie, an overweight thirty-year-old, fussed with her bleached blond hair. Under the overhead neon light fixture, her hair appeared to have the texture of straw. Al loved this woman's fierce personality, always with an edge. Of late, he realized she had softened and taken to mothering him since his wife, Mildred, died.

"No problem, no problem, none whatsoever, Deb," he said. "Thanks for asking. This'll do fine."

He glanced around again and noticed a third child. The three children sat with their parents at one of the larger tables along the wall to his back. Two older ones, a boy and a girl, played tic-tac-toe on the white paper tablecloth. The youngest, a boy, ignored his brother and sister and, instead, cuddled with his mother, nudging and fidgeting, waiting for Debbie to deliver their food.

Gazing at this familial scene, the old man pictured his daughter raising her own young family in California. He realized how much he missed seeing the kids after her husband, a Marine lieutenant, had transferred with the family to Camp Pendleton. The Corps had him scheduled to ship out to Afghanistan soon, and Al worried about his son-in-law.

Al hated to worry—about anything—and he disliked tension—in any form. He was a remnant of less turbulent times when countries on the other side of the globe weren't competing to prove the validity of his favorite astrologer and prophet, Nostradamus: that total world destruction would begin in the Middle East. No, Al preferred a more peaceful world. He fought the good fight of WW II and retired from violence to a quiet street in the suburbs to raise a family. All he ever wanted from life was a steady job, a wife who loved him, and children who respected him. He enjoyed those rewards for many years. Two years ago, he and Mildred sold their house in Westchester and moved into Manhattan, into a small one-bedroom apartment right across the avenue from the restaurant. Six months later, cancer took his wife. Now he struggled with the adjustment to having lunch alone.

Al stood and moved to the opposite side of his small table so he could watch the three lively children without straining his neck. From his switched position, he had the first opportunity to examine the parents with some focus. The father, a fortyish, rotund man, spoke with a slow-mannered drawl, and the mother, he observed, was Asian. An appealing woman, with midnight black hair, high cheekbones, and a slight frame. He guessed her to be Chinese. She appeared to be in her late thirties, although he could never be certain of a Chinese woman's age. He recalled how often they fooled him during his Army years while stationed in San Francisco. The women, he remembered, never looked their years.

The features of the three offspring were unmistakably Eurasian, possessing the clear, even-shaded, darker complexion, ovate-shaped eastern eyes, and raven-black straight hair. Yet the scene created by the children at their table was pure Americana. Al noticed their speech patterns, expressions, and tone were the same as he heard from his own grandchildren. The two boys looked like twins despite their age difference, and the chubby girl, whose body, unfortunately, favored her father's, appeared to be the oldest. Once their lunches arrived, their activity quieted.

Debbie returned to his table with his crispy chicken salad plate. After placing the dish in front of him, she said,. "Mind if I keep you company for a while, Al? Most of the lunch hour rush is over. I need a short break."

"No, no, no problem, Deb. Sit down," he said, shaking his attention away from the neighboring family. He had been musing about the number of oriental-Caucasian mixed kids he had seen in the past. Motioning with his head toward the group, he said to Debbie, "You ever wonder why so many of that racial mixture produces such beautiful children? They seem to end up with the best features of both cultures. Don't you agree?"

"To be honest, Al, I never gave it much thought. Mind if I smoke?" she asked, flipping open a pack of cigarettes.

"Naah, no problem, go ahead."

Debbie inserted a filter tip between her lips, and before lighting it, she asked, "But you believe that's so, Al?"

"Oh, yes. Yes, I do." He scooped a forkful of chicken salad into his mouth. Chewing for several thoughtful seconds, he swallowed and said, "You know, when I was a young officer stationed in San Francisco, long before I met Mildred, you understand, I got involved with this girl who had an Irish merchant seaman father and a Chinese mother."

"Go on, Al, you were never a bachelor. You and Mildred were married a hundred years."

He ignored her humor and continued. "Susan was a stunner; in fact, she worked as a photographer's model. Our relationship got pretty heavy, to tell the truth. Still, it didn't work out."

Debbie looked up and raised her eyebrows. "Sorry about that, Al."

"Yeah, well, that's ancient history now. For all her beauty, she wasn't happy about being a mixed race. She would have preferred being one or the other. She told me that once."

"Hmmm, weird," Debbie said between puffs. "Hey, you ever make the Haight-Ashbury scene in San Francisco?" She asked the question as though she had tuned in to a different conversation.

Al smiled, amused by her historical error. "No, Deb. You're talking about the sixties. I'm talking about the forties."

She lifted her head and squared her chin, trying to focus on her miscalculation.

He continued. "Some years later, I spoke with a mutual friend. He ran into her once in a restaurant in Palm Beach. She'd married well and was enjoying life in South Florida."

Debbie got to her feet when she spotted a late customer entering the restaurant. She looked around and sat back down when the newcomer went to the counter. "You got it, Marvin?" she called to the counterman. Marvin nodded. "So she found happiness in Florida, right? You sorry about missing out?"

Al studied Debbie's face. He thought he detected a knowing grin forming. "Yeah, well, as I said, it's history now. The sad thing is this fellow told me she had no children. Well, I got to wondering. Perhaps she had no interest in perpetuating the pain she sensed—real or not—in being a mixed race."

Debbie flicked her cigarette ash into the tray. "What pain, Al? What was so painful? She had a lot more going for her than I got. Palm Beach? Hey, I'd trade places with her any day."

He reflected on Debbie's question while he fixed his attention on the five people at the table enjoying the pleasures of ordinary family life. "You know, perhaps the pain was mine," he said, "Susan's reaction to her ethnic mixture might have affected me. I don't remember. It was so long ago." Something else popped into his mind and he turned back to the waitress. "You got to understand, Deb, her mother was born in China. She spoke very little English, and for that reason, Susan never invited friends home to meet her family. Her mother's inability to converse embarrassed her."

Debbie blew out a trail of smoke through her nose. "Gawd, what an awful thing. To be embarrassed by your own folks. What kind of daughter was she, anyway?"

"Well, for one thing, she was self-conscious about not fitting into either world. She blamed her parents. Not like those three over there. Sure, they appear to be happy children. But what about when they reach adulthood? I worry about it, you know. Will they find a more accepting world, one where the lines separating races blur?" Saying this, he considered the real question that had always nagged him. "But let me ask you something, Deb."

"What's that?"

"Should they blur, or should they remain distinct? I always reasoned it was selfish of mixed-race couples to have children, never taking into account how growing up mixed would affect the kids as adults."

Debbie took a deep drag on her cigarette and blinked as if she was trying to absorb his words. "That bothered you back then, Al?"

"Yeah, I guess it did." He paused and took another bite of chicken salad. "Hey, the offspring of these mixed marriages have no say. If they did, would they choose not to be born instead of growing up with the same resentments that bothered Susan?"

Debbie stared at him. "And maybe they wouldn't, Al." She exhaled through puckered lips, and thin circles of smoke formed over Al's head. "And maybe the world has got better. Maybe not. Who knows?" she added. "Listen, Al, I gotta get back to work now."

His attention had returned to the interracial family.

"Thanks for the chat," Debbie said. "And Al, remember, you missed one bus but you caught another. It got you to the same place, didn't it?" She walked away without waiting for a reply.

He glanced over at the mother cuddling with her young son and wondered about that first bus. He recalled how he couldn't catch up to it fifty years ago. Could he catch up today? No chance, he decided, and he left Susan in San Francisco once again.

SIGNS OF THE TIMES

"Not true, little sister, I do understand," Pam said. "I'm aware it's not easy for anyone to discover her fiancée is bisexual." She turned back to Cynthia, who'd been standing behind her in the tiny kitchen. "I'm not being insensitive. Then again, don't you suppose you've grieved long enough?"

When she finished loading the dishwasher, Pam closed the door and pushed the NORMAL WASH and ENERGY SAVER buttons. The appliance leaped into motion.

"The damn romance is over," she added. "Done with, for goodness' sake. Coffee?"

"No, thanks."

Pam steered Cynthia out of the kitchen and into the dining area of her compact one-bedroom apartment, back to the glass-top cafe table, and they sat. "You did say no coffee?"

"Not for me. It's late. I better be leaving soon."

She reached across and cradled her sister's hand in hers. "Listen to me, hon, you're twenty-eight. It's time to move on. I mean, after six months of monk-like existence, you need to do something about getting a life."

Cynthia took a deep breath through her nose, held it for a moment, and released the air through her mouth. She squeezed out a smile and said, "I suppose I am guilty of overindulging my breast-pounding prerogative."

"Of course, you are. Nevertheless, you can't keep beating up on yourself for making an error in judgment." Pam gave her hand a playful slap. "Even though you should have been perceptive enough to read the signs."

"That's the point. I didn't see any. Nothing, from the first moment I laid eyes on Oskar at the embassy party."

Pam recalled the letter from her sister explaining the origin of her painful ordeal. The Danish government had reassigned Oskar to their Paris embassy around the same time Cynthia's bank transferred her from their London office to the City of Lights. She met Oskar there at the party.

"Tell me again, who introduced you?" Pam asked.

"One of the officers of my bank—a Jean Louis somebody. I don't remember. Why?"

"Well, for God's sake, didn't this Jean Louis somebody know?"

"If he did, he didn't let on. Goodness, it was just a simple introduction of two people." She smiled. "You remember how liberated the French people are about sex? Paris is full of liberals."

"What attracted you to him? I mean, I still find it incredulous."

"Oh, God! Such a beautiful face. And...and the way he spoke ...that lilting sound Scandinavians have. What can I say?"

"That's all? I cannot believe just his voice was enough to entice you to move right in with him. Even before you learned to pronounce the name of his hometown. What was it, Genitalia?"

Oskar came from a small suburb of Copenhagen called Gentofte. Cynthia had mentioned it to Pam and how she'd struggled with the pronunciation from the get-go.

"Don't be funny," Cynthia replied. "You pronounce the name, Gen-tof-te." She was careful to accent the te the way Oskar had instructed.

Pam grinned, but her sister ignored her.

"Well, to begin, he oozed European sophistication. A lot different from the nerds I dated in London. And, he was so attentive . . . oh, God, I hate to admit it . . . especially in bed."

"Don't! Don't go there." Pam covered her ears. "I don't want to hear." She let her hands fall and said, "Now I understand why you were upset."

"Yes, and how about the large measure of embarrassment it caused me at the bank? Why do you imagine I returned to New York and went into hiding? Can you blame me?" A resigned shrug accompanied the obvious tone of desperation in her voice.

"No, although I do blame you for your annoying preoccupation with superficialities."

The corners of Cynthia's eyes pinched. "What do you mean?"

"I mean, there's more to the human condition than a beautiful face. Your selection criteria of men never reached below the surface."

"Am I really that way?" Cynthia sounded surprised.

"For as long as I can remember. Ever since you discovered boys. From your high school days, college, and even in grad school. Everyone you brought home—George Hamilton look-alikes. Not deep, except it didn't matter. That may explain why you didn't get the message from Oskar."

"Maybe," Cynthia said. "Maybe you're right."

Pam patted her arm and spoke softly. "Listen, I read about these unusual lectures over at the 92nd Street Y. Look into the program, why don't you? The series runs the gamut of a bunch of different topics. You know, practical stuff. You might enjoy them. Besides, it's an excellent forum to meet new people."

"Okay, I'll check it out. I promise."

* * *

Cynthia signed up for a three-lecture series. The first one intrigued her: Survival in New York City. She arrived at the Y with a renewed feeling of the future and was quite unprepared for her reaction to Barry Tomkins, one of the men in attendance.

The lecturer peered out over the classroom and announced, "Why don't we start by introducing ourselves?" He pointed to a young man in the first row. "Let's begin with you. Stand up and tell us your name, something about yourself, and why you chose this lecture."

He stood beside his chair facing the group, his hands clasped in front and his shoulders thrust forward, making him appear taller. "Hi, I'm Barry Tomkins. I hail from Akron, Ohio, and now I make Manhattan my home."

He brushed back a wisp of sandy hair in an affected gesture. Pausing, he looked around the room of faces. "I live in the Village and work for a major law firm in midtown, Brown and Steel. We specialize in all types of theatrical representations."

He reminded Cynthia of a contestant on *Wheel of Fortune.*

"Since moving here," he continued, "I witnessed the city go down the toilet. You know, dirty, dangerous, and downright hostile. I'm here to learn how to cope. I don't want to end up having to sing, Whyoh, whyoh, whyoh, why did I ever leave Ohio . . . ."

He finished the opening lines of the song from the 1953 stage musical, *My Sister Eileen,* and the group reacted with scattered laughter and applause. Cynthia's focus locked on Barry's face. She became hypnotized.

After several of the other attendees completed their introductions, the leader called on Cynthia. She looked up, startled, and rose to her feet. "Oh, I'm sorry," she said, swallowed, and recited, "Cynthia Fenyo . . . Manhattan . . . banking." Taking her seat, she returned her interrupted attention to Barry's face.

She examined his fragile good looks, his chiseled features, and his tapered build. It pleased her whenever his soft, tawny-hued eyes darted in her direction.

* * *

Unable to control herself, Cynthia's unleashed infatuation grew with intensity over the next twenty-four hours. Barry's image consumed her thoughts. She cast her eyes in both directions, finding it hard to believe she was there, standing on the top step of a subway entrance in midtown Manhattan, ready to pounce on him. She was a cheetah in the wild. A grieving victim one day, she thought, a stalking predator the next. She giggled at the mental picture and panned around to check if anyone noticed.

Barry gave his company's name during his introduction, and Cynthia found it on the internet. She guessed he would leave about five o'clock, and since he lived in Greenwich Village, she assumed he was likely to cross to the opposite corner for the downtown Eighth Avenue subway entrance.

She could see the facade of his modern office building and the revolving doors from the top step of the subway stairs. The avenue was heavy with rush-hour vehicles, and only when a bus caught the occasional traffic light was her sightline blocked.

Her thoughts raced as she stared across the avenue. What am I doing here? He's going to think I lost my mind. Cynthia rarely submitted to impulses as she had when she first met Oskar. While their relationship became intimate almost immediately, she hardly considered herself a reckless woman.

Even so, this current bizarre adventure was unfolding right off the top of her head, and she felt out of control.

She spotted Barry as he crossed the wide avenue in full stride in her direction, and only her locked grasp around the handrail kept her from bolting down the steps and into the bowels of the subway. She was sure he had seen her as he stepped off the curb to cross. If not then, at least a second or two before she faked the collision on the sidewalk at the top of the stairs.

"I'm sorry," she said, as she bounced off his shoulder.

He kept his balance and turned around. "Excuse me. I didn't hurt you, did I?"

"No, no, I'm fine." She faced him waiting for the moment of recognition. Then, not trusting providence, she blurted, "Barry?"

"Hey, you're Cynthia. Right? Last night's lecture at the Y." A warm smile appeared as he extended his hand. "You work in this area, do you?"

"No, no, I'm on my way to Lincoln Center to pick up tickets."

"Oh? Well, I was heading to P.J. Allen's right here on the corner. Twofers until seven. Want to join me?"

Cynthia hesitated and then gushed, "Oh, I would love to." She followed him into the tavern, her face beaming with her sense of victory.

"What a surprise running into you like this," he shouted over the din of the happy hour crowd. "Hope you don't mind sitting at the bar. I need to be somewhere by six-thirty. Not a lot of time. What would you like to drink?"

"A gin and tonic," Cynthia replied.

Barry ordered a Miller Lite. With an artful flair, he filled the Pilsner glass, tilting it as he poured. He set the bottle and glass down without spilling a drop. Cynthia stared at his meticulous performance, clutching her drink with both hands as if she needed it for support.

"Where did you say you were going when I almost knocked you over?"

Cynthia leaned in close. "Lincoln Center. To pick up tickets for the ballet."

"Right. Well, why did you get off at this station? Fifty-ninth Street, Columbus Circle would have been closer. No?"

"Guess I goofed." Her dishonesty became a distracting muscle spasm. She twitched on her barstool, swishing the plastic swizzle in her drink like an oar.

"So, you're a patron of the ABT?"

"I'm a fan," she said, trying to sound casual.

The conversation lulled while Barry took several sips of his beer. The P.J. Allen bar scene was happy-hour frenetic. Cynthia sat gazing at him until she became uncomfortable with their silence. Gulping air, she declared without provocation, "I was engaged once to a Danish diplomat stationed in Paris. He was their cultural attaché and a fanatic about ballet. Do you like ballet?"

"I used to. I'm much more into opera now. What are they performing?"

"I'm ashamed to say I'm not sure." Again resorting to invention, she added, "I'm just picking up tickets for a friend." She lowered her eyes hoping he would miss the lie.

"My, what a pal."

His voice sounded distant, and when she raised her head, she saw why. He'd become distracted by the tall, youthful barman at the far end of the bar.

Barry turned back. "I'm sorry. I thought I spotted an old friend. Anyway, how'd you enjoy the first lecture last night?"

"Very much. How about you?"

Relieved he changed the subject, she sat back, content to let him do most of the talking. Cynthia did not handle small talk well, but her initial awkwardness was disappearing. The second gin and tonic was taking effect.

"That's why they call it a self-help seminar," she heard him say. "Like the one last night. Supposed to help you deal with the dangers of living here in the Big Apple. You know, like what to do when traveling alone late at night."

"But I don't remember New York City ever being this threatening. Not that way before I left for Europe. An awful lot has changed in three years."

"Oh, you're right. When did you get back to the States?"

"Almost six months ago, but I've been a bit of a recluse since. Other than going to and from work, I don't get around much."

"Any particular reason?"

Overcome with a sudden rush of openness, she answered, "I guess you could say I was in mourning."

"Someone died?"

"No, no. Only my engagement." She said it and regretted the self-pitying sound of her words.

"Uh-oh! Pretty bad stuff, eh?"

Cynthia swiveled on her barstool trying not to look at him. "Yes, it always feels that way, although better I ended it when I did."

Barry stared, waiting for her to continue.

"It would have been worse later. That is, if we'd gotten married." As soon as the words were out, she realized the admission opened the door to a full confession.

"You make it sound as if it was preordained to fail."

"Oh, in this case, it was." She could feel the resentment of the last six months returning. "How can I put this delicately?"

He set his glass on the cocktail napkin and waited.

Cynthia paused, searching for the right words. Realizing there was no graceful retreat, she would handle it with humor. "You might say he was an equal opportunity lover. He turned out to have bisexual proclivities."

Barry looked down at his watch. "Hey, I gotta get going. I'd like to continue with this. Perhaps another time, but I'm glad we ran into one another."

He slipped from his stool and turned to help her down. Several standing patrons elbowed their way toward their vacated seats. Taking her arm, he threaded a path through the crowd toward the exit. They reached the sidewalk and Barry asked in an off-handed manner, "By the way, might you have met up with a Peter Sharpe while you were in Paris? We were roommates during his assignment with the British consulate here in New York. His transfer was quite unexpected, and we've kind of lost touch."

Cynthia blinked. Indeed, she remembered him. He'd been a friend of Oskar. Only Peter Sharpe had not been bisexual like Oskar. He'd been exclusively gay. "Yes," she responded. "I knew him." She thought she would choke on the words.

"Well, what a small world." His wry expression said it all. "Sure you're all right? You're aware Lincoln Center is in that direction," he said pointing with his thumb.

"Yes, of course. I was considering taking a taxi."

"That might be a good idea this time of the evening. Remember the survival lecture from last night?"

"You're right. See you next week, and thanks for the drinks."

"My pleasure." He turned and walked toward the subway entrance.

Cynthia stood riveted, unable to move from the curb. She didn't notice the red DON'T WALK sign flashing at her. When she stepped off the curb into the street to look for a taxi, the blaring horn of a bus chased her back.

"Good lord!" she gasped. "You really do need to read the signs to survive in this city."

THE GOLF GAME

"My two favorite pastimes are sex and golf. Although, as I grow older, I find myself assessing their order of preference." Charlie made that comment to golfing colleagues many times over the years. The quote always brought a laugh, but I believed he meant the words.

Charlie's undeniable passion was golf. During the evening of the club championship awards last month, I suspected he got carried away with his zeal. And it didn't stop there. But let me tell you what happened and you can judge for yourself.

At dinner, my wife and I sat at a table with Charlie sandwiched between us. He had arrived alone. Some serious ailment confined his wife to home; no one knew anything more than that. The whispers were the big C, but Charlie never talked about her condition. Even when she was in better health, I could not recall the last time she came to a club function.

Charlie and I played golf together in a regular foursome. More often than not, we'd end up playing as a twosome. The other two golfers in our group traveled a lot on business. Except for the occasional post-game beer in the clubhouse, my relationship with him ended at the eighteenth green. Our fierce competitiveness would not allow a close friendship to develop.

I'm a twelve handicap, proud of my honed game, and something of an egotist about my ability. I seldom minded giving him the required three shots a side. What drove Charlie was his propensity for one-upmanship, besides his passion.

At the dinner that night, swept up in the mood produced by the festivities, feelings of camaraderie among the celebrating club members, and three Beefeater martinis, he said something to me, which, after I responded, I was sure he regretted saying.

"Ralph, I love golf more than you do."

Of course, in retrospect, I realized the remark was innocent, not meant as a challenge. Yet I reacted as though he'd questioned my manhood. Charlie was expressing his deep reverence for the Royal and Ancient game. That's all. In contrast, my approach to the sport tended to be more clinical. Despite this, his inexplicable declaration incensed me.

"How the hell can you make a statement like that? How do you quantify the boast? What is it, the number of rounds played, the number of golf balls lost, the years playing the game? For Pete's sake, Charlie, how can you support that claim without providing some logical reasoning?" I'm sure my face turned crimson.

"Ralph, it's based on a feeling I have in my heart," he slurred in his inebriated state.

"Aah, bullshit!"

"Listen, give me time. I'll bet you ten dollars I can come up with a way to prove my point," he said, offering my wife a wink.

Certain the three martinis had taken complete control, I snapped, "You're on, damn it!"

* * *

All that happened more than two weeks ago. Since then, I hadn't given further thought to the challenge. When you consider his condition, I believe Charlie wouldn't recall much of the evening.

This past warm, sunny Saturday morning, as I drove the golf cart to the first tee for one of our many rounds as a twosome, my mind settled on the eighteen holes of enjoyment ahead.

I brought the cart to a standstill abreast of the ball washer. The chlorophyll scent of freshly cut greens and fairways permeated the air, filling our nostrils. Course ambiance was one of the things Charlie never failed to comment on during a round. He claimed it was an essential part of his love for the game. The manicured fairways and greens, the beautifully maintained shrubbery, the trees, and the flora—all those things turned him on.

"What'll we play for?" I asked, knowing he hated to bet on golf. He wasn't cheap, you understand. Betting distracted him. He would often kid about conceding the bet upfront, paying me the money before we teed off. As he was an able weekend player, the pressure of betting always cost Charlie strokes. I liked that.

He deliberated a moment as he stepped to the washer to clean his Top Flite. "How 'bout a two-dollar Nassau?"

Now, I don't know if you're a golfer, but a two-dollar Nassau is about as small a bet as most golfers make. Unless, of course, you're an old retiree playing in a regular foursome at a public links in southern Florida. There, you're apt to find fifty cents as the standard.

"Okay. How about a dollar for birdies and greenies?" I proposed, increasing the pressure a touch more.

"No sandies," he insisted.

"Fine, you want to play from the whites or the blues?" I knew he preferred the shorter white tees. He tended to overswing when playing from the blues. When he suffered an errant drive from trying to kill the ball, I would remind him, "Charlie, you can't reach the green in one."

"Okay, big hitter," he replied, attempting to keep a poker face, "we'll play from the blues. Except, you have to give me one more shot a side."

"Forget it, sport. We'll play the whites." I remembered that occasionally he could out-drive me by ten or twenty yards. I always had great difficulty hiding my irritation whenever he did.

"Lead the way," he said, gesturing to the tee box.

I moved into the teeing area between the two white markers, surveying the grass surface for a level patch with the fewest divots. After I found my spot, I pushed the tee into the ground. With the same hand motion, I balanced my brand-new Titleist Pro V-1 on top. Stepping behind the ball, I took a sighting on a target line and moved around into the address position. This pre-shot routine helped me maintain a playing rhythm. My favorite Callaway driver gripped in my left hand, I folded my fingers and thumb of the right hand into the proper position on the shaft and executed a smooth swing. The ball soared up and out like a fighter jet off a carrier deck, carrying almost two hundred and twenty yards on the fly. After rolling another twenty yards on the dry, firm fairway, the ball came to rest on the long, lush carpet of green just right of center.

"Nice shot," he praised as I moved by him and out of the tee box.

Once he placed his driver behind his teed Top Flite, Charlie wasted no time. He took the club back and around in a well-executed takeaway. His driver met the ball on the sweet spot, and the white sphere leaped off the clubface, depositing a crystal-pure metallic sound in the warm air. The drive behaved in flight almost identically to my shot. His ball bounced on the right side of the sloping fairway and rolled, stopping four yards beyond me, but in the long grass.

"Looks like you caught the right rough." I could not disguise my gloating tone.

I stopped the golf cart next to my ball. He stepped out, took a five wood from his bag, and walked into the rough to assess his lie. I chose a three-wood for my second shot. The ball sat up on the fairway carpet, begging me to strike it with precision.

"You're away. You hit first," he shouted over his shoulder. The away reference irked me, but then that was his intended purpose.

Most golf nuts love to torture listeners with a shot-by-shot description of each hole. I'll spare you. Suffice it to say the next seventeen holes progressed in exactly the manner as the first.

Both of us reached the eighteenth green in regulation with the match all even. Charlie needed four of the six shots I had to give him, and I'd gifted him more help when I shanked my tee shot back on the par-three, thirteenth hole.

A cavernous sand bunker bordering the right side of the large kidney-shaped putting surface of the eighteenth green started in front and carried around to the back. The left side of the green rolled down a small hill and into twenty yards of long grass. Beyond the rough, the perimeter fence that flanked the length of the course property separated the green from a main, busy thoroughfare. The clubhouse loomed in view one hundred yards ahead.

Charlie faced a ten-footer for a birdie. I had a six-footer. He would ordinarily putt first, but out of character, he signaled for me to go ahead. He said he wanted to take his time examining the undulating line to the hole. I saw no reason to object. If I holed out, it would have cranked up the pressure on Charlie, perhaps causing him to three-putt for a bogie. I missed my birdie by inches and tapped in for a par

He leaned over his ball, lining up his putt for some time. I stood to one side, staying out of his line of sight. We always observed the game's courtesies no matter how ferocious the competition became. He completed his preparations and gripped his putter. With the putter head suspended over the ball, I heard him say to no one in particular, "Seems to move left to right." The club stayed suspended over the ball, while I waited for him to drop it into the putting position. Instead, he released one hand and raised his arm to look at his watch. I stared in disbelief when he straightened and placed his ungloved right hand over his heart. Charlie stood at attention.

I noticed the source that provoked my companion's bizarre behavior and was astonished. He had caught a glimpse of a line of cars with their headlights on. They followed a gray hearse down the street and proceeded slowly past us. Charlie never moved until the procession went by. As the last car drifted out of sight, he resumed his putting stance.

I always considered Charlie a decent fellow despite our friendly rivalry and competitiveness on the golf course. He had an unquestionable sense of propriety. For example, I never caught him rolling the ball over when summer rules were in effect. However, his overt demonstration of respect for the deceased at this decisive moment in our game frankly caught me by surprise. Obliged to comment to my friend, who, only two weeks earlier, bragged about loving golf more than I did, I told him, "Charlie, you're amazing. There you are, standing over the most critical putt of the match, and you let yourself become distracted by a funeral procession." Twisting the knife, I added, "And I thought golf was your passion?"

"It is, damn it!" he shot back while continuing to line up his putt. "What the hell, we were married thirty-four years. That's the least I could do."

The initial shock sent me reeling. When I regained my composure, I stormed off on foot toward the clubhouse. As I passed our golf cart, I heard his putt drop into the cup, and I knew I had lost the match as well as the challenge. I turned my head to say something and stopped. Charlie was laughing.

A REASON TO SMILE

The words blazed across the front page of the newspaper: STEINBRENNER OWNERSHIP CONSIDERS SELLING YANKEES. Lynn had time to read only the article's lede line before the antique carriage bounced to a stop on the eleventh floor. Morris, the operator, something of an antique himself, shot her a look over his shoulder. "Eleven."

She tucked the folded paper into her DKNY tote bag, pulled out a Kleenex, wiped the inky smudges from her fingers, and turned to Morris.

"I wish they'd print these things so the stupid ink didn't come off."

Morris ignored her.

Lynn exited the car, pausing long enough to take one more shot at trying to make the curmudgeon smile, a game she played with him each day. "Hey, Morris, how 'bout them Yanks last night? Took extra innings to pull out the win.

Boston is a tough team. And now, maybe we'll be rid of the ghost of George. Did you catch the headlines?"

"Who cares?"

The grumpy reply was scarcely audible as the noise of the closing gate and door lopped off the old man's words.

It was hard to take umbrage with his acerbic manner. He came with the territory. Lynn liked to joke that you had to expect "a Morris," when you worked in one of the few office buildings on the Lower Eastside of Manhattan that still used manually operated elevators. She referred to these relics as the last frontier of daily personal abuse. Those remaining in operation were destined for self-service modernization sooner than later. Sad to say, the Morrises of this world were a doomed breed, facing certain extinction.

A traditionalist, Lynn preferred these ancient chariots. Their metal accordion gates and manual controls connected with her. She enjoyed watching the floor numbers race by on the exposed shaft interior while the car hurtled to its next port of call. The thumping noise made by the carriage passing each level beat a unique tattoo. Keeping track of the numerals flying by on the shaft wall was dizzying and fun. As were the bouncing stops when Morris misjudged his landings.

She pushed through the double-thick glass doors and into the offices of HARTE ADVERTISING. The modern design of the agency's portal was the only updated touch in the entire pre-war building. Thirteen tenants remained, and all opted to stay with the original Stone Age appearance: stenciled black letters on opaque, pebbled glass panels at the top half of the door.

A receptionist seated behind the large mahogany desk looked up from her typing. "Morning, Lynn," she said.

* * *

The time was one-thirty when Lynn spotted him. He stood in the corridor at the elevator, his eyes fixed on the ornate floor indicator above the painted metal door. He failed to notice her as she joined him in his vigil.

"Hiya, Dave."

He made a deliberate slow turn toward her. "Late for lunch, aren't you?" He was grinning.

"On the phone with the client. One of those marathon calls, trying to sell him on using your radio spots for the campaign."

"How'd you make out, ol' silver tongue?" His grin melted into an impish smirk.

Lynn fashioned her expression into a frown and stared at him for several seconds. She recalled, with secret pleasure, the instant attraction she experienced when the agency hired Dave to write copy on her account. Old school about mixing professional and personal relationships—in Dave's case, the temptation proved challenging—she never let theirs progress beyond an occasional flirty exchange. Even so, she did fantasize about him often.

"Hey, Shakespeare, you consider yourself pretty cute, don't you? Don't tell me you didn't know all along he was ..." Her words faded as the elevator's opening door revealed the craggy face of Morris.

"Down!" the operator's gruff voice announced.

Dave trailed her into the carriage, and they stood shoulder to shoulder. Morris pulled the handle to close the outer door and clanged the interior accordion gate shut. They started down without a word.

THUMP ... THUMP. The elevator spoke as they flew by each level. They watched in silence as the painted numbers zipped upward. Within a few seconds, the carriage ceiling light blinked twice and clicked off, pitching them into total darkness. The movement of the carriage slowed with an accompanying grinding noise until they bounced a few times and came to a full stop between the third and fourth floors.

"Uh oh, what happened?" Dave asked.

Lynn's eyes strained as they adjusted to the dark. She turned toward Dave's voice. "I have no idea. Morris, what's wrong?"

"Lost power," the old man answered. "Same thing last month when the generator suffered an attack of the crapolas. It'll come back on soon." He sounded unconcerned. Somewhere from the depths of the basement, a bell clamored for the building engineer's attention.

Dave turned to her, his warm breath on her neck. "You alright?" he asked.

"Oh, sure. This is fun. I mean, how many opportunities have we had to share a dark closet?"

"So you haven't told me. How'd you make out with the client?"

"Not too bad. I'll give you the details later—if we ever get out of here."

Initially, she wasn't sure, but when she felt it a second time, she knew. Flesh! A hand! His hand! He had taken the tips of her fingers in his, and slowly enveloping her entire hand, he lifted it—uncontested—to his mouth and kissed the soft heel of her palm. She snapped her head toward Morris, who she heard shuffling in his corner and flipping the control lever as he waited for the building engineer to restore power.

Convinced the old man could see them despite their blacked-out condition, Lynn tried to pull her hand away. "What would you do if I yelled rape?" she whispered into Dave's ear, attempting to keep the words between them.

"Cool down. Don't get so uptight," he replied, making no effort to whisper. "I'm leaving the agency, so it's okay."

"You're kidding, aren't you? Did you quit?" Lynn asked, certain the old man was listening.

"Yep. Gave my notice a few minutes ago. I was waiting around for you to break the news. The reason for this late lunch. I start on the fifteenth at FSB as a group head. Now I can beat up on five other copywriters."

FSB was one of the top ten ad agencies in the city. "Well, congratulations," Lynn said, and as the significance of his revelation sank in, she added, "Oh, right. Now we. . . ." Remembering the operator, she swallowed the rest.

"Of course, you nit," Dave said. "You don't suppose I've been standing here holding your hand like this because I'm afraid of the dark?"

"Oh, wow!" Her voice seemed to amplify with the absence of light.

In the next moment, the single bulb over their heads flickered back to life. Dave released her hand.

Wasting no time, Morris pushed the lever forward. The carriage obeyed and jerked downward, bouncing twice after reaching ground level. The old man folded open the gates. "Lobby," he announced as though the trip had been routine. He reached for the handle of the exterior door and pulled it, exposing them to the sunlit lobby.

They exited quickly. Dave took Lynn's arm and led her toward the door. "You know," he said, "this has been a good morning. We'll celebrate. I'll buy lunch."

Before pushing out onto the street, Lynn cut her eyes back over her shoulder. Morris stood outside the open elevator door leaning his shoulder against the wall. He was smiling.

"No," Lynn said. "Change that. This has been a great morning. I'll buy."

SWEET 'N' SOUR

Saturday morning and a stranger's voice fills the bedroom. The radio alarm, set for seven, cuts short Arnie's delicious dream. He lingers on his pillow next to his wife, Brenda, the details of his sex fantasy with his ex-wife, Carol, still fresh in his mind. Images come flooding back into his consciousness like a re-run of an X-rated movie.

Brenda, her body curled up around his rear, is emerging from her sleep. Arnie is positive his face will betray him when he turns over.

"You awake?" she asks in her soft morning voice.

"Yeah, I think so."

"Arnie. About last night. I guess I misread your signals. Probably too much wine. I'm sorry."

This bed is crawling with guilt, he thinks. "That's okay. You take the bathroom first. I'll put on the coffee."

He rolls onto his back and watches Brenda at the foot of the bed meticulously flick the straps of her sheer nightgown, shrugging it free of her slender arms and shoulders. The garment cascades down the shapely line of her body like the unveiling of a statue, gathering in a small pool around her ankles. Arnie fights a resurgent wave of guilt.

"Funny, the only thing red wine does for me is give me a headache," he says to her naked form as she disappears into the bathroom. "But no, not old Brenda," he shouts. Her giggle drifts back. He sits up and pulls on the fly area of his pajama bottom, looking for telltale traces.

Last night, as soon as they were under the covers, her hand went exploring. The mood was not there, and he doesn't know why. The last time they made love was two weeks ago, and last night is not the only time over these recent months he'd failed her.

Arnie's mind returns to thoughts of this past year of unemployment. Not only has it been an emotional roller coaster of unproductive job interviews, but his lack of income has produced a financial vacuum to his bank balance. The cumulative effect of both has smothered his libido.

Standing barefoot on the cool kitchen tiles, he measures three scoops into the fluted paper filter of the Mr. Coffee machine. The details of his erotic dream continue to tease. He stays alert, listening to the shower noises coming from a short distance away. The whooshing stops and he pushes his memory-off button before the bathroom door opens.

Brenda appears in the kitchen doorway. Her damp ash-blond hair is towel-wrapped. She holds a second towel around her neck, but she's covered nothing else. "Didn't you like the Cabernet last night?"

"Yeah, I did, although you know me and red wine—the headaches. Must be the preservatives they use."

"And the way I am with all wine," she says grinning. "Like an aphrodisiac."

"Rest assured, my lovely passion pit, I'm not complaining."

"We should get an early start, you know. It's a long drive and Philip expects us at the dorm by three. I hope we can fit in all his stuff. I don't understand why the kids can't leave everything over the summer. After all, they leave the place empty. Oh, and Arnie, let's not forget the checkbook this time. His room deposit for next year is due before he leaves."

Her tiny, slender frame rocks as she speaks. He stares first into her hazel eyes and lets his gaze wander. The simplicity of Brenda's sexual magnetism could always ignite his senses. Even in a crowded elevator, he likes to tell her. He remembers his nocturnal adultery and his head throbs with guilt. He's grateful when she reminds him to go shower.

The warm, pulsating water splashes his face as he puzzles over the meaning of his dream. He hasn't given a thought to this phase of his past life in over two decades. His mind time-travels back twenty years to visions of a brief but stormy first marriage: to Carol and their watery, wild sexual games in the shower; to a period when his fledgling business career was poised to take off. He remembers life with her as fast-paced and fun sometimes, despite their basic incompatibility outside of the bedroom.

Brenda opens the door to his steamy inner sanctum and a rush of cold air reaches him. Her words tumble over the shower's glass partition. "Arnie, pancakes or French toast?"

"Either is okay."

* * *

Scrutinizing their last bank statement over two cups of coffee, Arnie pushes the document to one side. He moves his chair closer to the table, where his foot can reach under to Brenda's lap. She massages his five toes, one by one, producing waves of shivers and a mixture of pain and pleasure.

"I can't recall a time when I felt so worthless," he says, eyeing the figures on the bank document. "And I thought I had it rough those two months I was out of work five years ago.

Remember? Before I got the job with Tele-Tronics? I wasn't facing age discrimination then."

"Sweetheart, I don't understand people's attitude about hiring someone over fifty. Shouldn't all your experience count for something?" Her strong fingers work swiftly over his gnarled big toe.

"Oooh! Not so hard. I broke that one in college. Arthritic as hell. Yeah, if I told you how many forty-year-old presidents I talked to over these last six months, you might understand how—"

"Forty? And they're presidents already?"

Arnie takes his right leg back and replaces it with the left. "Isn't that something? When I was forty, I was in middle management, looking for my chance to climb into the upper echelon before I hit fifty."

"Well, dear, you got there, didn't you?" Her fingers lace through the spaces between his toes with extra tenderness.

"Aaaaah, that's nice."

Brenda produces a warm smile.

"Yeah, a whole lot of good it did me. I make VP only to be turned loose a year later because the damn economy dived into the crapper."

"Honey, really! Do you have to use such—?"

"And, at the same time, the company gets crushed by the worse stock market this country's seen since the twenty-nine crash. I ask you, Brenda, when can you remember so many white-collar workers affected by the economy?"

"I can't, honey. Things will change soon, won't they? I mean, how long did the crash last?"

He yanks back his leg and bolts upright to his full five-eleven height. "By God, Brenda, people who couldn't face that crisis were jumping out of office windows."

"Arnie, you're not so depressed that you'd—"

"No, of course not, except if a job doesn't come along soon, we need to take some serious measures. I mean, I'm not entitled to unemployment anymore, and we're low on cash, down to our last five thousand in the savings account." His wild gesturing makes him look like a symphony orchestra conductor.

Brenda springs to her feet and moves around behind him. She rises on her toes to reach up to his shoulders and presses him back down into his chair. He bends over the table resting his head on his arms, while her hands and fingers are busy at work on his neck and spine.

"Ummmm . . ." he mumbles. "More at the base of the neck . . . yeah, yeah, that's it . . . ouch!" He stiffens. "Damn, that's sensitive."

"Oh, did I hurt?"

"No, no. It's great," he says, lowering his chin to his chest. Arnie's head dangles like a lynch mob victim while Brenda continues her massage. For several moments, neither one speaks. He savors his wife's loving manipulations and the moaning she emits in concert with her working fingers. He is certain she has closed her eyes and is enjoying his physical pleasure. His head snaps back again when he remembers the bank statement.

"Brenda, what would you think about selling our Disney stock? Not all. About ten thousand dollars worth, enough to get us through the next three months. Hell, Brenda, we need some relief."

Her hands rest on his shoulders for several seconds. "Well, if you assume selling it is necessary, I guess. But gee, Arnie, aren't we managing so far on my teaching salary?"

"Hey, you make decent money, but not enough to carry all our expenses and to cover Philip's tuition for his third year. Of course, we could ask him to take a semester off and work. I would hate doing that."

Brenda's hands fly from their perch up to her mouth like two released pigeons. "Oh lord, we couldn't do that!" she exclaims through her fingers. She takes a deep swallow and says, "Well, if we have to sell stock to keep him in college, I guess we have no choice."

"That's the way I see it, although I wish we didn't. Our portfolio is a major part of our retirement money, along with our IRA." Arnie gets to his feet and heads toward the leather sofa in the living room. "I'm going to catch the *Today Show*, see what the weather's going to be for the drive." With the TV remote in hand, he stretches across the sofa cushions on his back.

Brenda clears the table of coffee cups, breakfast dishes, and silverware and puts everything into the dishwasher. This is Arnie's chore, but in deference to his distracted state of mind, she takes over. After finishing, she approaches the sofa and Arnie lifts his legs out of the way. She sinks into the seat cushion at the far end and he plops his feet across her lap.

"When do you expect to hear about the Rhode Island situation?" she asks, without turning her eyes from the TV.

The position is Arnie's only live prospect, and he's aware Brenda dreads the idea of relocating. "Well, the last conversation I had with the division head was two weeks ago. He has a hard time deciding, worried the wrong decision will come back to haunt him. He'll drag it out as long as possible. Maybe another thirty days. I'm not holding my breath."

She rests her left hand on his right kneecap. With the thumb and forefinger, she kneads the top side of the bony mass. His leg jumps, then settles.

"Well, I can't imagine finding someone more qualified than you. How many marketing vice presidents can there be with as much knowledge about satellite transmission as you? They are going to select you. I have a feeling."

"Yeah, well, I hope you're right. Hard to tell with the way the economy has hurt the tech industry these days."

Brenda's touch makes its way up the inseam of his pants with deftness, playing with the welting under his thigh. The talking head fills the TV screen, but the images drift over Arnie's closed eyes.

"We won't have a tough time selling this apartment, will we?" she asks. "On top of everything else, I'd hate to take a loss."

"Not to worry," he mumbles. Then, as though the reality of her question has registered, he raises his voice. "Considering what we paid, we won't lose. The market is hot right now. Besides, we're not selling the place right away. At least not until I have assurances the position is everything it's supposed to be." He opens his eyes to look at her. "Damn it, Brenda; it's not a *fait accompli.* They haven't offered me the job yet—if they ever do."

"They will, dear, they will." Her hand disappears into his crotch and rests there.

His eyes re-close in surrender. He no longer hears the TV. Every muscle releases. His mind shuts down the way factory machinery does at the four o'clock whistle. Moments pass and he sits upright. He is smiling as he swings his legs to the floor, stands, and reaches back for her hand. Taking it, he pulls her to her feet.

"Wait a minute," she pleads. "I want to watch the weather report."

"The hell with the weather."

"Arnie, dear. Philip is expecting us by four."

"He'll wait, passion pit. He'll wait."

"Okay. If you say so, dear."

A BIRDIE THE HARD WAY

The near-disaster struck as I exited the halfway house between the ninth green and the tenth tee box. I stepped out on the gravel path with a large Pepsi in my hand and heard the screen door bang shut behind me just as the utility vehicle—a cross between a small pickup and a golf cart—swept around the corner of the wooden building. It missed me by the length of a putter; however, the soft drink I carried did not.

The dust veil created by the speeding vehicle separated me from the barely audible voice floating back. "Sorry, Mr. Carpenter."

My relationship with the greenskeeper went sour last summer, but I doubted it deteriorated to where Carl would risk an attempted manslaughter rap. The rift between us originated when I took him to task on the poor condition of several greens during a meeting of the golf club's Greens' Committee. After the incident, he scarcely acknowledged me.

"Damn it, Carl! Slow up, will you?"

I doubted the man could hear over the noise of the gravel kicking up against the vehicle's chassis. I glared at him as he disappeared beyond the cloud. Carl never looked back.

When I reached my parked golf cart, I set what remained of the Pepsi into the drink holder and grabbed my towel. What a jerk. He could have killed me. I should give him the cleaning bill, I thought. Yeah, that would clinch our falling out.

The darkening sky closed fast as I drove toward the tenth tee box. I was eager to finish my round before the slate gray clouds dumped curtains of chilly rain on my already moist trousers. I might have slipped into the leaky all-weather suit I ordinarily carried in my bag, except I remembered the garment was no longer there. Lucy, in her rush of generosity this past summer, donated it to Goodwill after she discovered the torn pocket and frayed cuffs.

"Didn't you tell me back in March you were going to buy a new one?" my wife asked when I complained.

"Yeah, except I won that rain suit in a member-guest at Winged Foot ten years ago. Damn! Winged Foot is where they played the eighty-fourth U.S. Open." She smiled and left the room. Ah, how did I expect her to understand? She didn't play golf.

Before teeing off this morning, I tried to lure the first assistant into a game, but he was busy with the monthly inventory at the golf shop. "Tomorrow's a better day," he said. "I'll finish by mid-day. We can tee off after."

"Okay, but it has to be tomorrow, or I wait until spring. My vacation ends this weekend. I go back to work on Monday, and I'm still looking to break eighty."

He smiled with the typical smugness of an assistant pro.

I was eager to complete that achievement to crow about it to my playing partners before our Saturday league got underway in the spring. Over this summer, my handicap had been trending down with the posting of the best scores of my golf career. I flirted with eighty twice. I was on a roll, and I needed to grab the ring while it was still reachable.

The clouds crawled across the sky, and I hoped I would not need the rain suit today. I worried because this was Halloween eve and the time of year in New England when the elements could play tricks of their own.

The temperature had dropped almost twenty degrees since yesterday's Indian summer weather. The damp, gray overcast sky might have gotten me down, except I considered any day spent on a golf course a good day, even if I had to tee off alone. Only nuts play this late in the year, but I had the eighteen holes to myself.

I drove to the tenth tee box and parked by the ball washer. A long stand of tall birch trees lined the side of the narrow fairway. The par-four hole doglegged to the right two hundred yards out. Any shot falling short of the turn ended up in jail. I examined my scorecard, pleased with the thirty-nine on the front side. It bolstered my confidence. If only I could be consistent on the back nine.

My drive was perfect. I caught the ball right on the sweet spot of my new Callaway driver. Damn! What did we do before oversized metal clubs?

The ball carried two hundred and thirty-five yards, landing in the middle of the leaf-strewn fairway well beyond the turn. It rolled to a stop dead even with the one-hundred-and-fifty-yard marker. A cluster of sycamores, their leaves turning varying shades of gold, framed the rear of the elongated green. I had a clear shot to the flagstick from there.

I inspected my lie, pulled out my five-iron, and moved behind the ball. A browned divot three yards ahead, surgically unearthed by a lazy golfer's slicing club and not replaced, became my line to the target. After several practice swings, I addressed the ball with a deep-centered concentration and executed a well-grooved takeaway. My downswing was swift, and as the ProV-1 and clubface came together, the white orb leaped off the sweet spot with a crystal-pure clicking sound. The ball rocketed into the chilly sky on a perfect trajectory toward the middle of the green.

I failed to notice a flock of blackbirds crossing overhead during my swing. The one I hit was in the center of the formation. The force of the ball ripped the bird up and around, leaving it suspended in the air for a split second. My deadly, dimpled Pro V-1 limped forward another thirty yards, its velocity spent, and landed on the fairway well short of the green.

The victimized blackbird became a soft bomb, plummeting earthward and landing with only a squishy sound. The remaining blackbirds broke off in mid-flight. They scattered wildly in every direction and filled the sky with flapping wings.

I drove the cart to the motionless feathered clump. A cursory examination confirmed the bird was dead. I consoled myself, knowing that it was a clean, fast kill. The remaining flock of blackbirds swirled overhead, cawing and swooping in wide, arcing circles above their fallen comrade. The scene they created appeared strangely Hitchcockian.

"I'm getting out of here," I said aloud. I drove my cart in a direct line to where my ball landed, slowing to scoop up the instrument of death on the go, and skipped playing the rest of the hole. At the eleventh tee, I recorded a six on my card and grimaced with the notion that my seventy-nine might have to wait.

* * *

Hank Simon, the well-liked locker room attendant, was alone when I entered. A short, fiftyish man with a handsome face and a full head of snow-white hair, he had worked at the club for over fifteen years. Hank's common sense coaxed many members out of a snit after a disastrous round. "Keep the game in perspective," he would tell them. "Remember, it's only a game." He offered those words many times during his years at the club.

"How'd you play?" he inquired as I opened my locker door.

"Not bad, considering." I pulled off my golf slacks, sticky from the soft drink, and folded them to take home. "I finished with an eighty-one. Damn! I should have broken eighty."

"So, what happened? Three-putt the tenth again?"

"Hank, you take great delight in reminding me of my problems with that green."

"Well, if you—"

"Yeah, I know. You tell me all the time. Skip the putting part, and I might come out okay."

"So?"

"Three-putted the seventeenth, not the tenth. I got a bird on the tenth, where I lost two more shots." I knew I was setting him up and couldn't help grinning. Hank's puzzled expression said I had him. "I took a double bogey since I didn't finish the hole."

He straddled the bench opposite my locker as though he expected a long story. "And so what happened?"

I related the tale of the blackbirds exactly as it occurred, making certain to include cawing sound effects. The greenskeeper interrupted our laughter when he appeared at the end of the row of lockers. We ignored him at first until Carl raised a club. That captured our attention.

"Mr. Carpenter," Carl said, "you lose a Ping-Eye sand wedge? Found the club making my rounds a while ago." He waggled the wedge as he spoke.

A tall, gaunt man, he wore a plaid hunter's cap and a matching woolen shirt-jacket that hung on his long body like a painter's drop cloth. He could have been a farmer from the Corn Belt.

"No, Carl. I use Hogans."

"Thought so. Just asking." He lowered the club and disappeared.

Hank shrugged, picked up my grass-caked golf shoes, and departed. I slipped out of my shorts, wrapped a towel around me, and padded off to the shower room.

The hot water was especially therapeutic as it pulsated on my shoulders and back. I replayed the round, hole by hole, visualizing the missed putts and my few errant shots. Despite the distraction on the tenth fairway, I played well. I came close again to breaking eighty. Maybe tomorrow.

I sat in front of my open locker, pulling on my socks. Hank reappeared carrying a shoebox.

"Here you go, Mr. C."

"What's this?" I said, pointing to the box.

"Your Foot-Joys, nice and clean."

"Since when did you start packaging them?"

He put the box down next to me. The cover sat on top.

"Mind if I don't use the box? The locker's overcrowded as it is."

I removed the lid without looking and reached in. "What in hell! Good God!" I recoiled as though my fingers had touched hot coals. The box fell to the carpet. The dead blackbird bounced from the container and came to rest at my feet.

Carl appeared from behind the row of lockers. He moved in quickly to stand beside Hank. In unison, their voices filled the room. "Trick or treat!" The two exploded with wild laughter.

I remained seated, my face warm with rising anger, and my eyes fixed on the two club employees. Their sophomoric behavior was beyond comprehension. They were a pair of Mutt and Jeff look-alikes bouncing around, slapping knees, and rolling eyeballs. I required several moments before my understanding of the bizarre scene came into focus. My annoyance faded as I released the air from my lungs. I was seized with sputtering laughter.

"Are you guys nuts?"

"You ain't mad, are you, Mr. Carpenter?" Carl said. "Found the bird out on the tenth fairway after you nailed it. I was going to trash it, except I thought it might be a gas to present it to you like the trophy of a big game hunter."

Hank picked up the narrative. "Carl came by earlier, looking for you, but you were still out on the course. He told me about the bird, and I suggested we make it a Halloween prank. Have a little fun with you."

"Well, your fun damn near gave me a heart attack."

"Honestly, we didn't mean to upset you," Hank said. "Figured you just might get a laugh out of it, that's all."

"Lose the thing, Carl," I said with a wave of my hand. "It ruined my game."

Carl shoveled the bird into the box and slapped on the cover. Seeing him with the bird-in-the-box tucked under his one arm, I realized the self-satisfied expression on his face in no way resembled the icy façade present over these past several years.

"Carl, I guess it took a dead blackbird to move us off of center."

He offered an outstretched hand. "You're right, Mister C," he said. "Sorry it took so long."

"Forget it. I'm happy it's over. But for a moment back at the halfway house, I thought you were out to get me."

"Guess I didn't realize how fast I was going. My bad."

After dressing, I stored my cleaned and unboxed shoes in the locker, clanged the metal door shut with a certain finality, and headed for the exit and the parking lot. "Later, Hank," I called out and left without waiting for a reply.

A light drizzle splashed my face on the way to the car. Lucky to complete my round today, I hoped my good fortune would hold out for tomorrow's game. Playing with the assistant pro was certain to turn up my level of play. I pulled out of the lot and recited my plea to the golf gods. "Please, this is my last shot to break eighty. No rain, no three-putts and I'll take my birdies without feathers, thank you."

THE FALLOUT

"**G**ood God, where the hell was your head? Didn't you see the damn car?"

He knew his wife would fire those questions at him when he arrived home. The only thing he could say would be, "Well, yeah, I guess I did, but what the hell, how often do you shoot and kill someone? My thoughts were still on that takedown of the drug dealer in the projects and not on my driving."

Narcotics Detective Gregg Fanning had been tailgating the SUV down the on-ramp to the Grand Central Parkway when he glanced back over his shoulder to check oncoming traffic. The right lane appeared clear. He hit the gas pedal hard, thinking the SUV had moved out. The impact was like watching a movie. It seemed disconnected, happening to someone else. He never heard the sounds of crunching metal and breaking glass.

Dazed for several seconds, Fanning hadn't realized his car had stopped. When he refocused, he spotted a hulking figure coming toward him, bent over like an NFL running back cutting toward an opening in the line. Except, instead of a football, he held a two-foot metal pipe.

For the second time within five days, Fanning reached for his duty weapon from the shoulder holster strapped under his arm. He stepped out of the car and shoved the barrel of his 9mm Glock toward his road-rage attacker. "Police. Don't move!"

The man raised the pipe. Now he was the quarterback with a wide receiver in his sights. He saw the gun pointed at his head and froze. Wide-set eyes stared out over a flat nose. Not in fear. In frustration. He was a boiling pot ready to explode. Fanning had locked a lid over him.

His dark complexion made Fanning consider he might be a Latino, or maybe from the Middle East. Uncertain the man understood English, he mouthed his words at him with a slow exaggeration. "Slowly lower your arm. Do it now!" The arm stayed suspended. "You understand what I'm saying?" No answer. Instead, the hulk rolled his eyes the same way Fanning's teenage son did when his mother caught him sneaking out the back door after dinner without finishing the dishes. The arm came down.

"Place the pipe on the ground. Do it now!"

He obeyed, and the pipe tumbled to the curb on the pitched roadway.

"Now step back five feet." The man hesitated. After Fanning shouted, "Now!" he responded.

The man was big, an easy two-fifty, maybe two-sixty, with an enormous neck, tree trunks for arms, and a head of black curly hair that crept down over his broad brow like a sprig of ivy. He wore athletic sneakers, faded jeans, and a clean white tee shirt with a Mickey Mouse image painted across his expansive chest like a mural on a small wall. Weightlifter, Fanning guessed.

"Step over to the curb and sit down," he commanded. The hulk inched back, sat on the grass, and folded his arms around his legs. Fanning returned his Glock to the holster, relieved he wasn't required to get into a wrestling match to control the man until a radio motor patrol arrived. At forty years old and 170 pounds, he was in fit condition. Fanning kept his five-foot, eleven-inch compact body in shape through regular workouts at the local YMCA. Yet he doubted he would have a shot against the moose in front of him, not only younger but close to half again his weight.

The noisy parkway traffic motored along, ignoring them. Fanning's golf shirt was sticky with perspiration. He damn sure didn't need the aggravation, another worrisome event to add to his life. He punched in 9-1-1 on his cell phone and waited. "Hey, yeah, this is Detective Sergeant Gregg Fanning from Queens Narcotics . . . ."

Once he completed the call, he turned to his attacker, "Unless you want me to cuff you, you'll sit there quiet like. Okay?" The man nodded and lowered his forehead to his knees.

Fanning picked up the pipe, surprised by its cool, smooth texture. The polished finish said it was new. He laid it on the back seat of his car and examined both vehicles. The minor damage to the man's mid-sized SUV amazed him. Fanning had drifted to the right seconds before his Ford whacked the SUV's well-protected rear bumper. The impact left the front headlight unit with a jagged mass of chrome and glass. With a little well-placed leverage, he thought he could pull the crushed fender free from the tire. He looked back at the hunched-over figure. "Hey, looks like I got the worst of the deal."

"Shoulda let you shoot me." The voice came from between the man's knees.

"How's that?" Fanning took several steps toward him and stopped.

"I said—aah, the hell with it. Never mind." The man lowered his head again.

Fanning waited while an American Airlines jet from nearby La Guardia Airport roared upward, climbing into a bank of low-hanging clouds. The plane passed over them, so close he smelled the jet fuel. The noise lessened, and he said, "No, tell me. You say I should have shot you?"

"Yeah, that's what I said," the hulk mumbled from between his knees. "Thought you were somebody else. Forget it." His voice was weak, but it was obvious he had no language problem.

"Shoot you? Why, man? You determined to die?" Fanning moved closer and picked up a musky scent of aftershave. "Why would you want to die?"

The hulk reached behind and pushed up. Fanning's hand went to his holstered weapon under his windbreaker. "Don't move! Stay right there."

The moose slid down, wrapped his arms around his knees, and lowered his head. Fanning had gone to his weapon to show he was not playing games. He considered for a moment what might have happened if the move had not worked. He knew taking down that huge body with physical force would be laughable, if not impossible.

The man raised his watery eyes. He tried to speak, but his heavy breathing choked back his attempt. Swallowing hard, he sputtered, "I mean . . . I mean . . . what do I have to live for?" He took a deep breath. "Since nine-eleven . . . my life . . . it's been a disaster. Lost my job, my two kids going through hell at school." He rocked his head like someone in complete disbelief. "They called my wife everything from a whore to God knows what, and by people we've known for years."

"Hey, you an Afghan?" It came out sounding as if Fanning had asked if he was a wizard.

"No way, man. I'm Indian. My family is from Delhi. Been here since '58. So has my wife's family. I grew up in Brooklyn. Graduated from Brooklyn Tech."

Fanning remembered Tech as a high school recognized for its powerhouse football program in the New York City area. He eyed the man's size again. "You play football there?"

"Yeah. Made All-City, too, like anyone gives a diddly shit these days."

"What's your name?"

With the heel of his hand, the man wiped the residual moisture from the corner of one eye. "Teddy. Teddy Vijay."

"How'd you get that name? Fanning said. "Teddy's not an Indian name, is it?"

"No. My given name is Teji Mahmud, after a squash champion my folks liked. I changed to Teddy in high school."

"Good move, man. Teji Mahmud doesn't sound like someone who could rip a person's head off on a football field." He smiled at his humor and cut his eyes to Teddy's face. He was smiling too. Fanning assumed the potential for more trouble had eased. Still, he wished an RMP from the local precinct would show up soon.

"You a New Yorker?" Teddy asked.

The question surprised him. Once someone listened to him speak, he couldn't imagine being taken for anything but a New Yorker. "Yeah, of course."

"Well, I am too. Born here," Teddy shot back. "My family may not have arrived on the Mayflower, but they lived here as proud New Yorkers. In fact, my father always told me, 'Teji, never forget you're Indian and a Muslim by virtue of your birth, but a New Yorker by the benevolence of Allah.' How's that grab you for Big Apple pride?" An inner light of enthusiasm seemed to envelop him as he spoke.

"Yeah, you qualify, alright." Fanning laughed.

"How long you been a cop?" Teddy asked.

What the hell is this, an interview? Fanning had his fill of questions from Internal Affairs after shooting the drug dealer, and now this from Teddy. He shrugged and figured that a running dialogue might help keep things cool for a while.

"Fifteen years," he said, running his fingers through his prematurely iron-gray hair. "Although, if they don't stop threatening my life the way they did this past week, I might not make it to retirement."

"Your life threatened? By who?"

"You mean, besides you? Some dirtbag drug dealer up in the Bronx tried to take me out. First time in fifteen years I had to shoot someone."

"First time?"

"Yeah. Gave me one hell of a scare seeing his gun pointing at me. I was lucky to get my shot off first."

"How'd you feel about taking someone's life?"

The image of his bullets smashing into the drug dealer's head and neck, shattering his skull, and severing the carotid artery, had haunted Fanning. The EMS technician told him the man died instantly.

"Bothered the hell out of me. I decided to take off these next two weeks to get through the trauma." He looked around at their two vehicles. "Some start to a vacation."

"You were justified in killing him. It was you or him, right?"

"The guy was garbage. Kind of what they got trashing the streets in Iraq these days. No one's gonna miss him. Still, taking someone's life is not easy."

"Part of being a cop, isn't it?"

"Yeah, and the one part I struggle with. I happen to believe life is precious, except if someone can't respect yours, he doesn't deserve to keep his."

Teddy winced. "I wasn't going to kill you."

"Well, you could have fooled me."

"No, honestly, I only wanted to hurt you."

"Yeah? So, trying to do that, you were willing to be charged with assaulting a police officer with a deadly weapon?"

"I didn't know you were a cop."

Fanning grinned. "What's the difference? Either way, it amounts to assault with a deadly weapon."

"I lost it. You rammed me. All I thought of was you did it intentionally—someone else using me as a scapegoat. I exploded. I decided no more crap from anyone."

"Is that why you came at me with the pipe?"

Teddy shrugged, and his enormous shoulders touched the bottom of his earlobes. "Yeah, I know. The fallout from nine-eleven, the craziness is driving me nuts. My life, my family, they're being destroyed."

"How come you lost your job?"

"Same bullshit. They had several contracts canceled. The Iraq war. Claimed they couldn't afford to keep on two computer programmers. One troubleshooter had to go. I was it. But I knew the reason was more about me being a Muslim."

"That's rough," Fanning said. "You're not the only one hurting from the fallout. How about the families of the three thousand-plus who lost their lives? That includes my kid brother."

"He was in the World Trade Center?"

"A firefighter trying to save lives until the south tower folded on him."

"I'm sorry. How old?"

"Twenty-six. On the job only four years."

Damn! Fanning thought. This bozo just tried to take my head off. Now he has me talking about my brother. Gerry called it taking the air out of the fire. His life was all about firefighting. Gerry apologized to me after passing the NYFD test. He said he felt guilty not following me onto the NYPD. I was relieved. No need for both of us to put our asses on the line every day. One ass in the family was enough. Yeah, sure.

Teddy raised his hips, trying to stand. "How about you? You blame everyone from that part of the world for nine-eleven?"

Fanning's hand slid back under his windbreaker. "Hold it there, Teddy. I told you to stay put. If you move again, I'm going to cuff you. Don't test me."

Teddy slid down into a sitting position again. "Sorry, man. Hard to sit still and talk about it."

Fanning understood. Every time he thought about his brother going down with the south tower, the image drove him wild. After nine-eleven, he wanted to nuke the whole Middle East. Weeks passed before he could speak of the tragedy with his wife without shouting, "Sons of bitches! I'd like to kill them all."

Teddy sat quietly. He sucked in a supply of air, and the ears of Mickey Mouse inflated. He exhaled and shook. Fanning suspected his road rage behavior was not his norm. Coming eyeball-to-gun barrel with his service weapon certainly woke up the guy if it didn't scare the hell out of him.

Teddy raised his head and said, "You didn't answer my question. Are you holding me responsible, along with everyone else from that part of the world?"

"Hey, man, it's hard not to lump all you towel-heads together." The towel-head crack slipped out, but Teddy showed no reaction. Fanning continued. "Those terrorists flying the planes, weren't they from different middle eastern countries?"

Teddy became animated. "Yes—I mean, no. They aren't sure where they came from. Some had stolen Saudi IDs. Did you know that? Later the real Saudis, whose identification they stole, turned up."

"Yeah, but don't forget, the al-Qaeda are Arabs, Pakistanis, Iraqis, and Kuwaitis. They're from all those countries, not just Afghanistan. And those captured in Afghanistan turned out to be from Bangladesh, Tajikistan, Uzbekistan, and a few of those other stan-countries that have an ax to grind with the US."

"You're correct," Teddy said. "However, no one from India."

He was right, and Fanning thought about the NYPD's profiling problems with African-Americans. "Well, I guess we have a tough time telling one Mid-East country from another."

"India is not a Mid-East country. It's in South Asia."

When Teddy said it, Fanning realized he'd been lumping together all those nations, holding them responsible for his brother's death— not just the Egyptian, Mohammed Atta, and his band of scumbags.

"So, Teddy, aren't India and Pakistan ready to nuke the hell out of each other with their own disputes? Like taking the rest of South Asia and the Middle East with them?"

"Not going to happen."

"I hope you're right, man, but you know what worries me? That Nostradamus got it right. He predicted the end of the world was going to start with the crazies in the Middle East."

"Come on, Islam's fanatical jihad has nothing to do with India."

"Well, you better hope Islam's nuttiness isn't catching. Nothing justifies the use of nukes by India or Pakistan. Or the use of pipes. You get my point?"

"Yeah, I'm sorry about that."

Teddy's expression said he meant it. He was not some low-life dope dealer apologizing as the cops locked him up for selling crack in a local schoolyard. Rear-ending him became the ultimate insult. It pushed him to the end of his patience.

"Well, what the hell were you doing with the pipe in your car? When you drive around with a two-foot metal pipe, hey, we consider that carrying a concealed weapon. And the way you tried to use it today qualifies as a certain nuttiness. Doesn't it?"

Teddy attempted to stand again. "Did you look in the back of my SUV?"

"Stay sitting, Teddy," Fanning ordered.

"I just wanted to show you the box on the back seat."

"I noticed the box before. What's in it?"

Motioning to the damaged vehicles, he said, "I was coming from Forest Hills Plumbing Supplies when all this happened. I'm converting a walk-in closet into a second bathroom. The box is full of pipes and sink fixtures."

Fanning decided Teddy wouldn't be a flight risk. "Show me."

A long line of vehicles had formed along the entrance ramp. Each car took turns feeding out onto the parkway, edging past their two parked vehicles.

Teddy stood and Fanning trailed behind him to the SUV. "Watch yourself," he warned as they came up to the vehicle. "Stay on this side. Don't touch the door, Teddy. I can see okay through the window."

The long packing box with the logo of Forest Hills Plumbing Supplies visible on the side rested on the rear seat. Teddy had left the top flaps open after he reached in to grab a section of pipe.

"Still believe I had the pipe to use as a weapon?"

Before Fanning could reply, the flashing strobe bar of the arriving police RMP cut him off. The vehicle pulled out from behind the line of crawling cars and onto the grass. Two uniformed officers jumped out holding their duty weapons.

"It's okay, guys," Fanning called to them. "Everything's under control."

Both officers, around the same age as Fanning's brother, Gerry, looked Teddy over, taking in his size and ethnicity. Fanning could anticipate the questions coming. He remembered his towel-head remark and cringed.

"You alright, Detective? We were told you'd been attacked."

"I'm fine, boys. The 9-1-1 dispatcher must have misunderstood. Nothing more than a minor fender-bender. My fault. Too quick on the gas pedal."

"Nobody hurt?"

"Nobody. We've been sitting here shootin' the breeze and haven't exchanged driver and insurance info yet. Give us a few minutes. After that, you can make your report. Then Teddy here can help me pull my fender off the wheel so I can drive it. Right, Teddy?"

A SMOKY CLOUD

True or false? Love at first sight happens. Or, let me put it another way: Can a bachelor of thirty-three experience the kind of love as defined by the readers of *True Romance Magazine*, the moment he sets eyes on someone?

"Oh, stop it, Harry. You're always falling in love. You're in love with love."

That was my older sister. I could count on her rebuke whenever I confessed to some recent infatuation—a new girl in my high school class who fluttered her eyelashes at me—a blind date in college that ended with a kiss. Little changed as I entered adulthood. I remained an insufferable romantic. Throughout my twenties, my string of over-the-moon relationships would support this indictment.

That noon hour as I sat at a table on the crowded second floor of the Playboy Club on East 59th Street in Manhattan, no one could persuade me my racing heartbeat and tremor-racked body were not signs of Cupid's arrow hitting the mark. It was that, or I had just suffered a goddamn heart attack.

I arrived late to the luncheon meeting with my British client, Major Peter Simone. The major chose the location for this occasion—not because it was his favorite spot to hang out, his after-hours watering hole—because it was. Oh, no. He had a plausible argument for selecting the club. We were meeting with Roy Dickerson, Promotion Manager of *Playboy Magazine.* On the agenda was an upcoming joint event with the publication and the client's product, Rose's Lime Juice.

"Harry, old boy," Peter said while twirling his Monopoly-man mustache. "This is an appropriate ballpark for our meeting. We're the visiting team." The major had become a dedicated fan of American baseball since his emigration from England.

Peter was a short gentleman with a round, jowly face, and a coiffed handlebar under his nose. Place a top hat on his head, a cane in his hand, and put him in a formal tuxedo, and he would convince anyone he had been the prototype for the famous icon of the board game.

He'd added a few pounds since his British Army days, and without question, he would now appear to his old comrade-in-arms as a "noticeably rotund, old chap." Despite the extra weight, he remained fastidious about his appearance. He maintained a neatly barbered head of gray hair, a color he would not allow to translate to his mustache. Those hairs he kept white.

Peter joined the membership of Manhattan's Playboy Club on opening day. The first one appeared in Chicago in 1960. Later, clubs sprouted up not only in Manhattan but also in New Orleans, Los Angeles, and elsewhere. Only a small percentage of key holders ever frequented them with any regularity. The reasonable charge of twenty-five dollars per year made membership an irresistible lure, an affordable status symbol with many traveling executives. Peter succumbed to this bargain-basement enticement like a lawn needing watering.

In the past, I would always suggest other options whenever he wanted to meet for a drink to discuss business. I disliked going to The Playboy Club. The scene was too glitzy and plastic for my taste. The Bunnies belonged in the FAO Schwarz wind-up toy section. On this day, however, I failed to influence his decision, and like a good soldier, I followed the major's orders.

Because of the horrific midtown traffic—nothing out-of-the-ordinary during a workday in Manhattan—I arrived ten minutes late. The challenges of the more aggressive cabbies were beyond what my little Pakistani taxi driver could handle. He tested my fast-paced New York City temperament on the trip from my mid-town advertising agency to the Playboy Club on 59th Street. Each time a Madison Avenue bus pulled away from the curb, Khalid found himself behind it.

Taking the stairs to the club's second level, I felt rushed and irritated. I was in no mood to conduct business. The Hostess-Bunny at the podium greeted me with a rehearsed graciousness.

"I'm meeting with Roy Dickerson," I told her. She smiled, pointed to his table against the far wall, and I huffed past a sea of luncheon diners to my waiting host.

"Sorry, Roy," I said, taking his extended hand. "Traffic was a bitch." I turned to my client and nodded. "Major, you look well." I pulled out a chair and sat.

Peter was unconcerned and delighted by my lateness because I had provided him with more ogle time. A happy marriage did not deter him from indulging in some harmless mid-life fantasies.

Roy turned around and raised a hand to summon our assigned Bunny.

"What are you drinking, Harry?"

My attention traveled to my client. "A gimlet, of course."

I was catching my breath when I reached into my jacket and pulled out the near-empty pack of Marlboros. With the filtered cigarette in the corner of my mouth, I rummaged for my Zippo.

"Hi, I'm your Bunny, Nicole."

I raised my head, and as she came into focus, Bunny Nicole had a Bic lighter flicked alive and held under my cigarette. Instead of drawing in, I stared, the Marlboro dangling between my lips. Two pools of dark hazel eyes reflected my stunned image as she leaned in. My throat constricted, choking off any attempt to speak. After several seconds, I heard a loud pop as my bemused mind returned to the present moment.

Red-faced, I allowed her to light my cigarette. "Thank you," I whispered, thinking, what the hell just happened?

Bunny Nicole remained standing, her eyes fixed on me, waiting for my drink order. I stared like a moth at a flame. My voice became hoarse. "Oh, a vodka gimlet and a pack of Marlboros, if you don't mind."

"Right away, sir."

She dashed off toward the service bar, and my focus stayed on her cotton Bunny tail. I was a high school freshman sitting at my desk opposite the prettiest girl in the class.

"Earth to Harry. Where are you?"

My attention remained somewhere out there.

Peter raised his voice and repeated the question.

I shook my head and looked at my companions. A flush of red appeared on my face and neck.

The major smiled. "Do you suppose you might wipe your chin and stop drooling before they throw us out? You're a bit out of character, old boy, don't you think?"

The character mentioned referred to my usual calm, all-business demeanor. Peter often teased me about it, claiming I sat through meetings and presentations with executives at Schweppes like someone listening to the reading of a will.

"I'm sorry, guys. She has to be the most beautiful Bunny in the club."

"She's new," Peter offered. "No time to develop a barracuda persona," the term used to describe the Bunnies who worked at the club during the nighttime hours.

Those rabbit-eared delights were notorious for their aggressiveness. They could shame any customer guilty of entertaining prurient thoughts into excessive ordering, thereby fattening the check. Round melons peeking out from immodest constraints, the Bunnies would perform the famous Bunny Dip while placing drinks in front of you. The arresting effect encouraged substantial gratuities at the end of the evening—the sole aim of the barracuda Bunny. The daytime Bunny suffered no such reputation. Most of their customers were executives enjoying a working lunch. Not like horny old Peter.

Something happened when I gazed into Bunny Nicole's dark eyes. The skimpy costume played no role in my reaction. Had she been wearing a flannel shirt and combat boots, the effect would have been the same. Her raven black hair, pulled back and held by a velvet headband, created a charming backdrop for the faux Bunny ears clipped to the band. A narrow white collar and black bow tie graced her otherwise naked throat. Her oval face, perfect nose, and pouty mouth reminded me of someone. I had my answer in a flash: Ali MacGraw, the actress of *Goodbye Columbus* fame.

Before Bunny Nicole returned with my drink and Marlboros, I made my pitch. "Roy, my good buddy," pawing at his sleeve like a kibble-starved puppy, "I would love to get to know her. Can't you figure out something to make that happen?"

"Come on, Harry. The club doesn't allow Bunnies to date customers. They'd fire her faster than a rabbit could reproduce."

My resolve was unrelenting. I continued to press. "What time do you think she gets off work?"

"Hell, I don't know. She works the day shift. You figure it out."

I received some helpful clues from the few innocuous questions I asked Nicole each time she arrived at our table. With a coy smile, she confessed she lived somewhere in downtown Manhattan and took the subway home. That was enough.

* * *

I'd guessed Nicole would leave the club around five. With a surprising burst of optimism, I ducked out of my office early and dashed to my apartment in nearby Murray Hill to change clothes. As I pulled off my tie, I glanced into the mirror on top of my bureau. What the hell are you doing? I asked the reflected image. You're the guy who never asks a girl for a date once she declines your first overture. So damned self-protective. I found no rebuttal to that bit of self-criticism. With an unprecedented urge to commit social suicide, I jumped into a pair of jeans, put on a sports shirt and my blue blazer, and headed for the door.

The adventure I was about to launch started on a positive note. I caught a taxi at my corner with a driver who turned out to be an aggressive Hispanic. The Cisco Kid maneuvered through the congestion of cross streets and clogged avenues like the taxi was invisible, and dropped me off at 59th and Fifth Avenue, one hundred yards west of the Playboy Club's entrance. I remembered the closest subway stop was at Fifth and 60th Street. During my taxi ride back to the club, I had calculated Nicole would walk to Fifth Avenue, turn north, and head to the 60th Street subway entrance. If I guessed wrong, I was poised to sprint in any direction.

I took a position on the corner for some time, scrutinizing patrons as they exited the club. Early in my vigil, I realized that someone had me on his scope. Now and again, the security man stationed at the club's entrance would shoot a wary glance in my direction. His charge was to prevent any lovesick key holder from harassing a Bunny upon leaving the club.

The corner of the St. Regis Hotel on Fifth Avenue served as my hideout. If I saw Dick Tracy look in my direction, I would duck out of sight. Once I thought the coast was clear, I would edge my head around the building for a peek. All the while, I worried Nicole might slip out and head east toward Madison.

After some time, I checked my watch. I had spent an hour and a half in one spot with no assurance my doggedness would not end up being anything but an exercise in frustration. Mystified by my determination, I decided to invest another half hour. Fifteen minutes later, fate handed me my reward. Nicole exited the club and walked toward Fifth Avenue. I retreated out of the view of the security man and stood facing the avenue with my back turned. She reached the corner and continued north up Fifth. I counted several beats before I bolted, reaching 60th Street as she began her descent into the subway. Suddenly I was Sir Walter Scott's Lochinvar rescuing the fair Nicole.

> *O young Lochinvar is come out of the west,*
> *Through all the wide Border his steed was the best;*
> *And save his good broadsword he weapons had none,*
> *He rode all unarm'd, and he rode all alone.*
> *So faithful in love, and so dauntless in war,*
> *There never was a knight like the young Lochinvar.*

"Nicole," I called.

She stopped midway down the steps and did a slow turn. She was smiling, calm, and self-assured.

"Hi," I squeaked. "Remember me? Ah . . . I waited . . . ah . . . I hope you don't mind. Do you think we could stop for a cup of coffee somewhere before you go home?" Now I was a twelve-year-old at my first school dance.

The smile remained. "I'd rather have a drink, but not around here. I can't risk being seen by anyone from the club."

Her words sent my heart pounding. "Terrific. Where should we go?"

"I live in the Village. Why don't we go someplace down there?"

"Lead on, Macduff," I said.

"Who?"

"Sorry. A misquoted line from Shakespeare's *Hamlet*. I can't contain my euphoria."

That earned me another beautiful smile.

Nicole started down the steps. I followed, and in my rush, almost tripped. Only the handrail saved me from certain humiliation.

Homebound riders crowded the subway car, pressing in on us from all sides. We faced each other, holding on to the center pole. The car was steamy hot, and the train raced downtown over age-old steel tracks making a loud clacking noise that prevented any opportunity to carry on a conversation. The upside was it provided me with a twenty-minute close-up examination of the face that transformed me into a love-struck fool. During the journey, her dark eyes would flash up, settling on my face, and igniting a warm glow through me.

"Let's make a quick stop at my apartment," she said as we ascended to the street level at the West Fourth Street station. "I need to change clothes, if you don't mind. Then we can go somewhere in the neighborhood."

She lived on the third floor of a brownstone walk-up in the middle of a short thoroughfare in the heart of Greenwich Village. I waited outside the building in the waning daylight, rolling her name over my tongue several times. I developed a passion in college for the sound after reading Fitzgerald's

Tender is the Night. The character of Nicole Diver singed my heart, and the prospect of a Nicole of my own made me tremble.

She reappeared wearing cocoa brown slacks and a yellow cotton pullover, her lustrous dark hair brushed and worn shoulder length. Incredibly, her beauty appeared enhanced.

"I know this little bistro, The Ninth Circle. Let's go there," she suggested. "It's a short walk, a great light menu, quiet, and we can talk."

I remembered the place as a famous steakhouse that seriously rocked in the '60s, playing host to a slew of the artsy and literary crowd. Folks like Janis Joplin, Jimmy Hendricks, Charlie Mingus, Norman Mailer, and George Plimpton, among others, gathered there to drink. By the 1970s, the number of celebrities dwindled to a low level, as did the restaurant's popularity. The owners sold out, and overnight, under the new proprietors, the bistro turned strictly gay before they sold it again.

Now in its third incarnation, the place was a friendly, low-keyed neighborhood destination on Tenth Street right off Greenwich Avenue, a five-minute walk from Nicole's apartment. The hour was early enough that only a scattering of diners occupied the tables across from the bar area. Still, I didn't want our conversation intruded upon by the loud group of two-for-one regulars watching a Mets game. I asked for a table in the back. The perceptive host, observing my moonstruck expression, accommodated my request.

"How long have you been at the Playboy Club?" I asked as we settled into a booth. With little chance to talk during the subway ride downtown, the question was all I could think of to begin my overture of sophisticated banter. I assumed my query was innocuous enough and didn't label me as a dweeb, fascinated with push-up bra-wearing Bunnies.

"It'll be a year next month," she said. "But wait. Tell me. How did you come to be on that corner when I passed you? Or were you waiting for me?" Her slow-forming grin was a giveaway.

"Busted," I said, my face warming again. "That security guy out front had his eye on me. He warned you, right?"

"No. He never said a word. How long were you waiting?"

"You don't want to know."

"Yes, I do. How long?"

My conflicted reaction demanded a choice: be mortified or brave. I opted for bold. "How about an hour and a half?" I confessed, keeping any hint of self-consciousness out of my tone. I sat back and gestured with open palms. "But look where we are."

A waitress in tight spandex leggings and a blue denim button-down man's shirt, hanging to her knees, arrived at our table. "Hi, my name's Sammy. Would you like to see a menu?"

I nodded, and she dropped a pair of tri-folds on the table.

"The special tonight is prime ribs . . . your choice of—"

Nicole interrupted. "Thanks. Just give us a few more minutes."

"Oh. Okay—sure. What would you like to drink?"

I looked at Nicole. "Vodka tonic," she said.

"Bacardi rum and a splash of Roses, please."

Sammy acknowledged the order with a nod. "Be right back," she said and disappeared toward the service bar.

Nicole scanned the restaurant. "I'm glad we're here early. This place becomes a zoo around nine."

The practice of placing small baskets of peanuts on each table as a centerpiece accounted for the shells littering the floor, giving the place an atmosphere of deliberate casualness. I eyed the peanuts and smiled. "Beats a cup of coffee uptown."

"Normally, I wouldn't have responded. But you impressed me with your courage. I mean, to wait around like that. You couldn't have known how long I'd be, or how I would react. Suppose I ignored your invitation?" she teased.

"I would've headed for the Queensboro Bridge."

"To go home?"

"No. To jump off."

Nicole raised her dark eyebrows.

I smiled. "To be honest, I considered you might blow me off, but I had to take the shot."

She regarded me with a somber curiosity.

"Hey, when you believe the prize is worthwhile, you go all out."

She laughed.

Sammy returned with our drinks and set them down. "You ready to order or need a little more time?"

"Give us a few more minutes," I said. "I need to find out who this girl is before I buy her dinner." I glanced at Nicole. "You never know. She may be an imposter."

Sammy left the table, and our conversation continued with the usual get-to-know-you type questions.

"Tell me, how did you become a Playboy Bunny?" The moment the words were out, I realized the question sounded lame. I was sure every first date since she donned the ears and Bunny tail led off that way.

Nicole took a deep breath through her nose and exhaled through her mouth. Yes, clearly, she'd been asked that before. Her reply rolled out with an easy spontaneity.

"Fates, the daughters of necessity. Plato," she said. "See, I read the classics too."

"Touché."

She flicked a shelled nut in my direction as though to emphasize her next point. "I was waiting tables in a small bistro in Greenwich Village, getting paid peanuts. One of our regulars was a Bunny. She took a liking to me and told me, 'Girl, why don't you get your butt up to the Playboy Club and ask for an audition? You can make three times the money.' It sounded tempting, so I auditioned, and they accepted me. I went into training, and here I am."

"Have you always lived in Manhattan?" A dumb question, I realized. Few people spend their entire life in New York City unless they are one of the Rockefellers. "Sorry, I should have asked, where are you from? Everyone in New York is from somewhere else."

"Connecticut—Fairfield County. I grew up there. Moved to the city two years ago."

"Never married?" I asked with a slight hesitation. Her response came fast and with a forceful tone that sounded like the slamming of a door.

"Not even close, thank you."

Sammy caught my eye, and, fearing she might grow impatient and lose interest when the place got busy, I suggested to Nicole that we check out the menu. "Are you hungry?"

She opened the menu without looking. "I'm up for something light. The Cobb salad is quite good here. I've had it before."

"Will that be enough?"

"Yes, fine. I try not to overdo my intake unless I'm depressed. Then I pig out and put on weight. The club management frowns on that, as you can imagine."

"I take it your choice of the salad means I haven't depressed you. That's a relief." I raised my arm to flag down Sammy. When Sammy arrived, I told her, "A Cobb salad for the lady, and I'll have the London broil sandwich. Oh, and two more drinks, please."

The evening went well. A simple invite for a cup of coffee morphed into a long and pleasant dinner spent learning about each other. Before the night's end, we covered the full gamut of family, education, travel, pet peeves, likes, and dislikes— everything worthy of mention. Nicole had two brothers, one older and one younger. Her mother and father divorced some time ago after a rocky fifteen years of marriage. She spent her childhood growing up in Norwalk, Connecticut. Life was a mixture of highs and lows living under the roof of her parents. I was certain she would reveal the details of those highs and lows during future dates, but for now, I was too far gone to probe further.

Eleven-thirty arrived before we could bring ourselves to leave the restaurant. We talked about going to dinner the following week, and she suggested I call to confirm before settling on a date. After saying goodnight at her door, I taxied uptown to my Murray Hill apartment, filled with excitement. I was back in love.

* * *

Wednesday morning, Roy Dickerson called me at my office. "Hey, any lunch plans today?"

"I do, Roy. Sorry. A working lunch with my creative team here at the agency. Not something I can postpone. Too many bodies involved."

After a long pause—I thought he hung up—Roy spoke in a voice that rang with uncertainty. That was something coming from the self-confident, straight-talking promotion manager of one of the world's most-read publications.

"Well, er, then, I guess . . . ah . . . I mean . . . I'll have to handle this over the phone. I was hoping to do this over a couple of gimlets."

A level of concern washed over me. Was there a glitch in some of the promotion details we discussed at the Playboy Club on Monday? Maybe the timing. I hoped there would be no reason to delay. I had budgeted the promotion for the first quarter, and I couldn't push it back to another time.

"What's up, Roy?"

I heard an uncomfortable laugh. "Damn it, I feel like the uninvited relative." He laughed again. "But this morning Peter asked me to handle the situation, and here I am."

"Okay," I said. "What's going on?" I was certain a disaster was about to befall the promotion. I got up from my desk and walked to the door to close it. If things became heated, I didn't want to startle my secretary seated outside my office door.

"Harry, after you left the club on Monday, I mentioned something to Peter. You know, about the Bunny you fixed on during lunch. He thought what I told him was funny. It might have ended there, but for the fact that on Tuesday morning, Nicole—the Bunny, that is—showed up at my office needing to speak with me."

"She did? What about?" My red-flag antenna leaped to attention.

"Yeah, she did. Surprised the hell out of me. She wanted me to know about your rather unorthodox ambush outside the club. The dinner you two had down in the Village."

"Roy, I don't understand. Why would she need to come to you about that? Did someone from the club see us and report her? Is she in trouble?"

"No," he said with a chortle. "It appears you are."

"How so?"

"Let me start over, Harry. I know you'll have a ton of questions. You see, I have known this Bunny since the day she started at the club a year ago. We did a photo shoot for the magazine with her and the four other girls in her training class. I picked up on it immediately. She sensed I did."

I turned my desk chair so that I could gaze out my window across Madison Avenue. Roy's voice sounded like a father explaining the birds and the bees to a young son. "Picked up on what?"

"Listen, the girls who become bunnies . . . you know, they aren't always what they seem."

Now the alarm went sky high. "So she's married, despite denying it."

"No, no. Well, some of them are. Not in Nicole's case. She is very single. What I'm referring to is their sexual bent. A few of them, as the saying goes, go the other way. Not something we like to advertise."

My reaction to such an unthinkable statement was to laugh. "You must be kidding."

"That's why she came to see me. Aware I was already on to her, she wanted my help to short-circuit further contact with you. She was afraid to face you with the truth, worried you would be angry with her. Nicole feared the misunderstanding would upset the magazine's business relationship with you. Even get her into trouble with the club."

I slammed back into my chair and almost dropped the phone. I could feel myself reaching for air, trying to find logic in the hours Nicole and I spent together Monday evening. "Damn! She liked me. We got along great."

"You're right, except your intense attention scared her. She knew it wouldn't develop into an easy friends-only relationship. She didn't want to hurt you."

"Wow! Let me catch my breath." After several gulps, I said, "Roy, thanks for the heads up. I appreciate the call. I'm disappointed. What else can I say?"

"So we're good? Roy asked with a note of relief.

"We're good."

"Okay, Harry. We'll grab lunch soon. Bye, bye," he said, eager to end the call.

I stared out the window across Madison Avenue for some time, waiting for the throbbing in my temple to ease. A smoky cloud appeared between two office buildings, somewhere over New Jersey. From behind me, a female's voice coddled my ear. I turned to look at the intercom speaker. Instead, what I heard was my sister: "Oh, stop it, Harry. You're always falling in love. You're in love with love."

STEELER COUNTRY

The wooden booth aggravated his hip at the spot where the bullet fragment remained—the shot in the ass that gave him a partial disability from the NYPD after fourteen years on the job. It was the first saloon Frank Daly had been in since he went dry. He felt stupid drinking Coke from a mug.

The booth's location allowed him a clear view of the front door. Sociable beer drinkers filled the place, the type of folks who refer to each other as "old-timers," something you would expect of the residents of a rural Pennsylvania town. And Beaver Falls was a rural town.

A thick haze of cigarette smoke choked the air and mingled with the saturated, stale aroma of beer. An old, fat Wurlitzer jukebox lit the front end of the long antique bar with a rotating sequence of colorful hues while dispensing polka tunes that added to the tavern's character. Bobby Vinton, the Polish Prince, belted out one of his patented ethnic melodies. The ambiance was an odd throwback to the saloons of the past, warm and friendly. The one thing missing was sawdust on the wide-planked floor.

Halfway into his soft drink, Daly spotted a tall man enter, take a quick look around, and go to the bar. He watched him bend across to whisper to the bartender. The man fit the mental picture Daly had formed earlier during their telephone conversation. He was certain the old guy was Raymond Burns. The one surprise? His height. Burns was a skyscraper.

A plaid shirt hung on his bony, gaunt frame. His baggy khaki trousers once sat on his hips a lot better than they did today. He looked lost in his clothes, and he gave the impression of a once-powerful man, now used up. Gray wooly hair stuck out clown-like from beneath both sides of a baseball cap with STEELERS stitched across the peak. Daly recognized the shape of an inhaler device, the top showing under the flap of the breast pocket.

Ray Burns approached the booth, shuffling his oversized feet. He was the image of a dog-tired mail carrier. His left hand grasped a mug of beer. He held it level, taking care not to spill.

"Frank Daly?"

Up close, Daly could distinguish traces of the young Airman from the picture his client supplied, a handsome face despite the few age lines.

"Yeah. Thanks for coming, Ray. Please sit down."

The man nodded, slid across the bench opposite, and swung his long legs under the table. Their knees collided.

"Sorry, these damn things weren't meant for . . . would you prefer a table?"

Burns's head twisted on his goose-like neck to survey the alternatives. He squinted as if weighing the advantages.

"Yeah . . . well, if you don't mind."

They headed for a small two-seater along the back wall. Settling in, Burns noted Daly's Coke. He did not comment, but his soft, penetrating eyes did the asking.

"I don't drink anymore," Daly confessed, the words rolling out without hesitation. As though Burns expected him to provide further clarification, he added, "Been AA for more than a year." He tried hard not to appear apologetic. The man's understanding smile surprised him.

They sat a while without speaking. The wheezing sound made by Burns' breathing punctured their silence. Daly tapped his toe, keeping time with the polka tempo coming from the Wurlitzer before he realized Burns was waiting for him to begin.

"First, can you explain how you knew I was here? I mean, out of curiosity."

Burns smiled. "You talked to my daughter today at Sylvania Hills Cemetery. Works there. Called me soon as you left. I told her she needed to let me know if ever someone comes nosin' around about my father, Raymond Senior."

"She aware why I was nosing around?"

"Only that her grandfather left a bit of unfinished business, and people are tryin' to lay claim to property he owned."

"After all these years?"

"She don't ask lotta questions, Mr. Daly."

This time Daly smiled.

"The name's Frank, and I have a few questions of my own."

He tipped back in his chair and folded his arms across his chest. He figured he might as well start with the sixty-four-dollar one.

"Are you Amy Chatsworth's father?"

Daly didn't need to ask. He had the required proof from his visit to the V.A. office. Perhaps he wanted to hear him say it—see how it sounded.

"Don't really know. The word of a girl I never seen don't make it so, does it?"

"Why would she make it up?"

Ray Burns raised his beer, took a mouthful, and stared down into the mug as if he considered chug-a-lugging the rest.

"Sometimes," he said, holding the mug to his face, "people have hard-to-understand reasons."

"Not so here, Ray. Amy's motive is simple. She would like to find out who her father is, learn something about him, and perhaps even meet him, if possible. You know, put the nagging mystery behind her, and fill in the piece of her life's puzzle missing for almost thirty-two years. That's the only reason she hired me."

"She's not looking for somethin' . . . to get somethin' out of—?"

"You mean money? Nothing like that, Ray. Amy is a wealthy woman. Married well. She's not looking for anything. Only a chance to learn who her father is."

"I was thinkin' more about settlin' a score, somethin' like that."

A burst of laughter carried back from the front of the tavern. Daly cut his eyes to the cluster of celebrating beer drinkers. Leaning into the table, he said, "Sorry, I don't follow you."

"She's gotta believe I abandoned her mother. That it was my doin' not goin' back."

"Not for a moment. The background report she supplied me indicates she understands what happened. She holds no bad feelings. None."

"I . . . I don't get it then . . . why . . . why would she spend all this time tryin' to locate me?"

"Ray, I told you why." His bewildered expression would not disappear.

"How'd she find where I live? My military records?"

"Not quite. She had your Air Force serial number, but nothing more. The State Department would not tell her anything. When she discovered the international network called Birth-Search, she contacted them. Within no time, she received your address here."

Burns frowned. "The letter she wrote to me? I answered and told her we buried the man she was looking for in Sylvania Hills Cemetery. Guess she didn't believe me."

"That's why I checked you out. I found the deceased was Raymond Burns Senior, too old to be her father."

The man took several deep breaths, picked up the mug, and took a swallow. "Frank, you married?"

The question pulled him up short. Burns asked it as if he had just run into an old Air Force buddy.

"Yeah . . . well . . . I mean, for the moment. I'm about to be divorced."

"Kids?"

Daly stiffened against the back of his chair. "Boy, fifteen, name's Travis. Listen, Ray—"

"Live with you?"

"Well, no, with his mother. Listen, Ray," he repeated, "no one I spoke with today knows why I was looking for you. You got nothing to worry about."

He wasn't sure Burns was listening. The old man fixed his gaze on the bottom of his emptied mug.

"If you don't want Amy to contact you again, I'm sure she'll oblige, except, in my opinion, you might want—"

"How's he takin' the whole thing?"

"Oh, fine, as I told you, she holds no—"

"Your son."

"Who?"

The question confused Daly for the moment. The man's focus had remained locked on Daly's own family problems.

"Oh, you mean Travis?"

Daly felt he was losing control, but he realized Burns' interest in his son sounded genuine. He welcomed the opportunity to talk about his troubles with Travis.

"Tell the truth," he began, "not too well. I'd always had a tight relationship with him. Now, since the separation, Terri has shaken the connection."

"How so?"

"Oh, filling him with all sorts of stories . . . you know . . . making me the heavy, blaming me for everything, that I wouldn't cut back on my drinking, as if it was a realistic option . . . that I'm an absentee father and husband. Now I'm worried about losing him." The words flowed out as if someone had turned on a water spigot.

"What's your son like?" Burns asked, encouraging the spillage.

"A good kid. Likes sports, and plays a fair third base. I haven't seen him in over a year, not since the night I showed up at the house on his fourteenth birthday."

"How come?"

"He was throwing a party. I don't know where the hell Terri was. Damned if I don't find a house full of kids sucking down bottled beer."

Burns gave a knowing look. "That's today's kids, I'm afraid. Wantin' to grow up so fast."

"Well, seeing them through my own bourbon-fogged eyes, I must have gone ballistic. Chased everyone home. That did it for him, I suppose. Me too. I joined AA right after. Not a drop since. Until I pass the first real test, I'll hold off telling him."

"Guess he's important to you." Burns looked toward the bar, waving his long arm like a flagpole in a stiff wind. "Need another of whatever you're drinkin'?"

"No. No, thanks. I'm fine."

The barman delivered another mug of beer and left.

"My family's important to me, too," Burns said. "Always been."

Daly wanted to say, Amy is your family too, but only by a technicality.

"Been married over thirty years," he said. "Three children and six grandchildren. You met my youngest daughter today. We're a close family. They all live in this area."

Daly visualized a Norman Rockwell Thanksgiving Day dinner at the Burns's home with the old man poised at the head of the table, holding a mammoth-sized turkey on a serving platter, ready for carving.

"Ray, you've no legal obligation to Amy."

His wheezing, quiet for a time, now intensified. He caught his breath, and Burns said, "I regret what happened back there. I'm sorry Amy's grandparents interfered with her mother's life. I loved her. Would have married her. Can't change anythin' now."

Daly saw him twist against the back of his chair. For a moment, he thought Burns would stand up.

"Don't blame Amy tryin' to find me, but comin' out in the open ain't gonna serve no real purpose. My wife, my children, I don't reckon they'd understand. Frank, you ain't got nothin' if you don't have family. Damn if I'm ready to risk losin' them."

The voice came from a man under siege. His emphysema breathing shortened and came in rapid intakes. The table shook beneath the weight of his large, flat palms. Daly decided Ray Burns and Amy Chatsworth would never meet.

"Listen, Ray, Amy hired me to find her father. I'm here. What happens now is up to you two. You have her address, don't you?"

Burns's eyebrows scrunched down over his squeezed eyelids. When the man opened them, his beaten expression disappeared. "You got a picture?" he asked in a firm tone.

Daly slipped the photograph from the folder and re-examined the woman in the picture before handing it across the table. He could see Ray Burns's features in Amy Chatsworth's face.

After a brief, detached examination, Burns dropped the photo as if it had burst into flames. Seconds later, he picked it up again. He shifted his long body to capture maximum light from the wall fixtures at his back, and then he brought the photo up to his face.

Daly sat watching. At the front of the tavern, a pair of old-timers danced to the music drifting back from the Wurlitzer jukebox. The tune carried over the noise from the bar to their table. ". . . little things mean a lot," warbled Pretty Kitty Kallen, the '50s songstress. Funny, he thought, that blast from the past was on my mother-in-law's list of favorites. In the early years, whenever she was at the house babysitting Travis, she would sing him off to sleep with the song.

"Looks like her mother," he heard Burns say. "Of course, it's been a long time."

"She get nothing from you?"

"Maybe my pointy chin . . . a bit around the eyes. She's mostly her mother, much as I remember."

The old man continued to examine the photo while Daly stared over the man's shoulder, out into the haze of cigarette smoke that circled overhead. Daly looked toward the long bar and noticed the New York Jets poster over the cash register. Strange, he thought. This was Steeler country. Then he remembered Beaver Falls was Joe Namath's hometown. He smiled, recalling the Jets General Manager, Weeb Eubank, and his contract signing of Joe in 1965, and all the resulting overblown media hype about the new Jets' birthplace. They made it appear as if the town was some sanctified Brigadoon of pro football, the Nazareth of all great quarterbacks.

Daly turned back to the old man. "Ray, you ever watch Joe Namath play football in high school?"

Burns eyed him with a quizzical look, his absorption with Amy Chatsworth's image interrupted by the query. He placed the photo on the table and pushed it across.

"My son's a Jets fan," Daly explained. "I have the feeling he's going to ask me that question when I arrive home after I tell him about you."

The old man grinned. "I did, many times. But, Frank?" His fingers rested on the photo. "Can I keep the picture?"

THE COME-FROM-BEHIND HORSE

The hard process of re-connection began last week when Claire telephoned. "Call Billy," she urged. "See him, please." My sister enjoyed more understanding and tolerance of the man than I did.

I had no contact with Billy in ten years. Not a phone call, a letter—nothing! Not until he surprised me by showing up that morning at my apartment building. I had left for work, and the doorman told me later that a Billy stopped by.

Back as far as I can remember, I called my father Billy. That never seemed odd. To call him Dad, Pop, or anything father-like would not have felt right. Everyone called him Billy. Growing up, whenever someone asked why I referred to my father by his first name, I would always laugh and say, "How else do you address someone who drifts in and out of your life with no more frequency than the meter reader from the electric company?" After I returned from Iraq, I fell into calling him Dad. I figured my change of heart had something to do with surviving combat.

"Are you kidding, Claire? You want me to phone him? After what he pulled—"

"Stop it, Nick!" she shrieked. "Stop being so damned stubborn. What in God's name do you suppose he was doing this morning, taking a nature walk through the neighborhood of Forest Hills? Billy is trying to reconnect with you. He has something to tell you, you thickheaded mule, and afraid if he telephoned, you'd hang up."

You got that right, I thought. I shifted the receiver to my left hand and grabbed a pencil. "You must know what he wants."

"Yes, but you should hear it from him."

"Let me think about it. Okay? He still works for that bus company in Queens?"

"Of course, he does, for heaven's sake."

"And living in the same place in Woodside? Same telephone number?"

"Yes," Claire answered, this time softening her voice.

* * *

My relationship with my father, as much as I tried, was never close. I was five when my parents split. Claire turned seven a week before he left. Thereafter, my father's contact with us became painfully irregular. For example, some people cannot ever arrive on time anywhere. In Billy's case, it was not a question of being late. Oh no. In most instances, he would never show up. As children, we found it difficult to understand, and harder yet to rebound from—impossible when he dangled prospects of a glorious adventure our way. This sense of rejection continued as adults, fueled and reinforced by every broken promise.

In retrospect, my purposeful exorcism of Billy began fourteen years ago. It was our first chance to spend time together after I returned from my tour in the Middle East. We were splitting a mushroom pizza and a frosty pitcher of Budweiser in one of Billy's usual hangouts, a local tavern called Rizzo's. The tavern's long-deceased namesake was a brassy, round Italian who, Billy vowed, used to make the best pizza in the world. As a pudgy toddler, I had reminded him of the rotund pizza maker, and he would often refer to me as his Little Rizzo. He told me that once, long after the baby fat disappeared, in a rare moment of tender expression.

"So, Nick, you decide yet what you're gonna do?" He sounded more curious than interested.

"Been accepted at Hofstra University," I told him. Assuming he might believe I was laying financial responsibility at his feet, I added, "But don't worry, I have enough saved for at least the first two years." He missed my sarcasm.

"Wadda ya gonna study?" he asked, taking time to chew between words and puffs of cigarette smoke.

"I'm considering English. A liberal arts major is the way to go since I don't intend to become a lawyer, or an accountant, or anything that boring."

"English? Thought you could speak it already."

"Funny, Dad. English Lit. You remember. Shakespeare, Milton, and all those other high falutin' Greeks."

"Huh? Oh, yeah. *The Music Man*, right?" He smiled, enjoying his small gotcha. Broadway shows, especially musicals, were among Billy's few healthy passions.

"Caught me," I said, continuing to play his game.

"English, eh? You gonna teach?"

"No. Maybe go into advertising."

"You wanna be in advertising?" Billy pulled hard on his Marlboro, squinting deep in thought. He let a mouthful of white smoke engulf his face. "Friend of mine, he's got a print shop," he said through the cloud. "He can teach you the business." Billy looked around the tavern with frantic urgency, twisting one way and the other until his eyes explored every corner of the restaurant. His quick movements came close to toppling the glass of beer in front of him. His head stopped swiveling, and he said, "Thought he might be here."

Billy had friends, many friends. They were important people to him. He could launch me into a printing career if I wanted to go that route. I tried to explain that printing was not advertising, at least not the end I was interested in. Told him I wanted to trade on my Army experience as a combat photographer, go into film production and make TV commercials on Madison Avenue where I wouldn't be getting my ass shot at every time I pointed a camera. Then, someday, try my hand at directing.

"You need college for that?"

"Well, yeah. I mean, you go to college for an education, not to learn a practical trade."

"Learning printing, isn't that education?"

I could think of no answer he would accept, so I stayed quiet. He gave up, shrugged, and we finished the pizza in silence.

Fast forward to our relationship during my four academic years, which I can summarize as an occasional beer and pizza, and a trip or two accompanying him to his favorite racetrack. If we sprinkled it with the usual high percentage of no-shows or cancellations, we would arrive at the breaking point where Billy succeeded in blowing me away. Despite a long history of disappointments, I expected this would be when my father would disrupt the pattern. I was getting my B.A. degree, and I thought for sure he would boast to his pals on his job at the local bus company, "Hey, my kid's graduating college next week."

"Ceremony gonna be at the school or someplace else?" Billy asked when I called.

"Outside on the main quad. I understand General David Petraeus is the guest speaker."

"General who?"

"Petraeus, Dad. David Petraeus. Used to be one of Obama's advisors. State, I think."

"CIA," Billy corrected with a chuckle.

"Whatever. I'll mail you your ticket later today."

"Okay, sure. Ah—your mother comin'?"

The passing of over two decades since their divorce had not made it easier for Billy to talk about his ex-wife.

"Of course, she is. So are Claire, Grandma, and Gramps. I have five tickets and I've included everyone. After all, when the hell did anyone on either side of our family graduate college?"

"No one ever graduated college. You're the first."

"That's what I mean. It's a big occasion."

"Sure is."

"So you know how to get there? The college is off Hempstead Avenue—"

"I know, I know. I've been out to Nassau County before. Fact is, last time, some goddamn seven-foot state trooper in mirrored aviator glasses pulled me over on the expressway for speeding. I wasn't doing over fifty-five. Let me go with a warning."

"How'd you manage that?"

"Told him I was friends with Bill Brennan, Precinct Commander of the 103rd in Queens."

"Okay. We'll meet you after the ceremony. Get to your seat early, at least a half-hour before, because the place is going to be a mob scene. Try not to get a speeding ticket."

"Thanks. I will."

"By the way, we're all going out for a celebration dinner afterward. I want you to come too. Okay?" I was pushing it, but I figured my timing might be good.

"Yeah, sure."

Over two thousand graduating seniors, their relatives, and friends made the quad look like the movie set of *War and Peace.* I spotted the family in the crowd minutes before the diploma processional, but I could not find Billy among the sea of faces.

Soon after the ceremony, I realized I'd guessed wrong about how high on his list of personal priorities the celebration of my academic achievement would place. Billy failed to show, and he never called to explain. Several months later, I learned the reason. My mother let it slip.

I had stopped by her apartment for my periodic treat of her home cooking, and the talk got around to my college graduation. "Do you think Billy might have been too uncomfortable with the idea of . . . you know . . . with you being there?"

"Nonsense!" she said with a clear note of anger in her tone. "That was your father being your father. Nothing's changed. He received a last-minute call from one of his drinking cronies with a tip on a horse. They went to the racetrack."

"You're kidding!" was my spoken reaction, yet I don't know why it shocked me. I rose from the table, walked to the window, and stared out into the blackness. "How did you find out?"

She offered no response. Instead, she began clearing the table. I waited. She finished and looked back at me with a cheerless expression. "Claire. He told her he forgot the date. Billy had received the call to go to the track, and he said yes without thinking. My guess is he was too embarrassed to phone you to apologize."

I fought the urge to scream, but I knew what I had to do. It was not even a question of choice. I resurrected my childhood hate, closed Billy out of my life, and remained resolute throughout the next ten years. I made this impulsive decision with a finality that surprised even me. Once made, though, I suffered no remorse, or, in any case, none that I would allow to surface.

* * *

So here I stood ten years later, at the door of The Dragonseed East, one of my favorite neighborhood Chinese restaurants, prepared to accept my re-connection with a man I thought I had written off forever. Billy would have been more comfortable meeting at one of his usual checkered tablecloth taverns, but I insisted we meet on my turf. I picked this place because the menu offered traditional Chinese dishes and not the newer, more popular spicy Szechwan cooking. Billy's shaky digestive system would not have survived that cuisine.

I arrived five minutes early and spotted him at the table in the corner I had reserved. He was wearing a tie—a fact that, by itself, was not so significant. He would always wear one under a V-neck sweater whenever we went to the fights at the Garden or, on those rare occasions, to the racetrack. "Never can tell if you're gonna run into somebody important," he would explain. However, on this night, he had draped his hound's tooth sports jacket over the back of his chair. Our reunion had to be a special occasion for him to rescue his only jacket from the closet. A thought crossed my mind. Perhaps he had elevated my ranking of importance a notch or two. Then again, he could be setting me up for a touch. In either case, I was flattered.

"How long has he been here, Chen?" I said to the restaurant owner.

"Oh, maybe fifteen minutes, Mister Nick," the man replied. "That table okay?"

"Perfect, Chen. Thanks for saving it."

I approached Billy, and he dropped the curly crisp from his hand, stood, and raised his arms to embrace. The gesture surprised me. I was a kid the last time I had any real physical contact with my father.

"Nick, Nick, thanks. Thanks for coming. How the hell are you?" He held me against his chest for a few uncomfortable seconds.

"Fine, Dad," I said, pulling away. "Any problem finding the place?" The smell of aftershave and cigarettes reached my nostrils.

"Naah, of course not. Used to have the Continental Avenue route when I drove for the bus company. Remember? I'm familiar with this neighborhood." He sat down, lifted his wineglass, and made a face. "Damn chink restaurants. No Miller Lite."

"Sorry about that. The food is good, though. You'll like it."

He wasted no time ordering, unwilling to be adventurous despite my urging. Billy devoured the spare ribs and moo goo gai pan with little conversation except for his inquiry of the waiter.

"How's ya Chinese beer? Taste anything like American?"

"Ah, very good," the waiter assured him. He decided to take the risk.

While we ate, Billy appeared self-conscious, making several forays with his index finger to ensure the tip of his napkin stayed tucked over the top of the knot in his tie. The main course disappeared, and a young busboy collected the bowls and plates.

"What's going on with the job? Still taking pictures of advertisements?"

"Filming television commercials, Dad. Moving pictures, not photos." I sensed the familiar irritation. It still irked him I hadn't followed his career advice. Had I listened, I would have skipped college, learned the printing business, and today I might be working for an engraver of fancy wedding invitations.

The waiter returned to take our selection of vanilla, chocolate, or pistachio.

"Want another beer?"

"No, thanks." He bent into the table and whispered, "This stuff will take the rust off your pipes. Listen, Nick, something I gotta tell you, speaking of pipes."

"Before you do, Dad, let me ask you a question." I pushed my chair out from the table.

"You gonna ask me about the day . . . your graduating day. Right?"

"No, no, that's ancient history now." I winced at the reminder.

I pulled back up to the table, leaned in on my elbows toward Billy, and rested my chin on my hands. "When was the last time, before tonight, you touched me? Can you remember?"

"You mean, like hit you?" He appeared confused.

"No. Not that way. I mean, touched me with affection." I studied the man's face for his reaction. My directness surprised him. These were uncharted waters for both of us.

The waiter's singsong voice interrupted. "Vanilla, chocolate, or pistachio?" He had remained standing at the table's edge, an obedient soldier waiting for his marching orders.

"Sorry," I said. "I'll take vanilla. Dad?"

"Nah, nothin' for me."

The waiter departed, and I turned back to Billy, who had reached for the pack of Marlboros in his shirt pocket. He stopped when he spotted the restaurant's signage prohibiting smoking.

"I ask because I just remembered the last time it happened. Tonight, when you hugged me, I had a flashback."

The lines around his eyes crinkled in tandem, and creases raced across his pained brow. He tilted back, folded his arms over his chest, crushing his tie, and waited for me to speak. I remained motionless, trying to recapture the scene.

"I was eleven years old. A bitterly cold night in January," I said, setting the scene. "I had the flu, and it laid me up for several days, in bed with a raging fever. Mom was having trouble breaking it. You came over. I don't recall how you got there or how you found out. I guess Claire told you. Anyway, you showed up, and I remember you sitting on the side of the bed, rubbing me down with alcohol, patting my chest, my back. You were very gentle, worried the alcohol was too cold.

That was the closest I'd ever felt to you, the most warmth you ever displayed toward me."

"Yeah, I remember. I was worried. You were one sick kid." He flicked his thumb and forefinger in a nervous tic. "That the last time I touched you?"

"The last time," I confirmed. "Can you tell me why?"

He forced a smile and said, "Wasn't it the last time you had the flu?"

I drew an exasperated breath. "I guess so," I answered without changing my expression.

The waiter's appearance halted the conversation. Billy shifted in his chair. He cut his eyes to the front of the restaurant, toward the door. His hand went to his pocket with the Marlboros, then stopped and returned to his lap. The waiter placed the ball of vanilla on the table, flanked by the check and obligatory fortune cookies.

Billy turned back to me when the waiter disappeared. "Hell, Nick, I don't know why. Us living apart those years didn't give me too many chances to hug you the way you wanted. Not that I didn't want to. Hell, you kids were the only worthwhile things in my goddamn screwed-up life."

My anger bubbled while he stared into my face, trying to read my thoughts.

"Nick, you believe I love you and your sister, don't you?" In his uneasiness, he drew a deep, quiet breath.

"Yeah, guess I do. That's never been too obvious, however. At least, not obvious in the way you value your friends."

His reaction, a nervous laugh, turned into a hack. His face flushed as he tried to control a phlegm-filled cough.

"You okay?"

Billy nodded as the cough eased. His red eyes leaked moisture.

"Sure, my friends are important to me, Nick. Of course, not the same way as you and Claire. It's just . . . well . . . ." His voice trailed off as he erased the tracks of tears with the heel of one hand. "Why the hell you mad at me?" He reached for the metal pot of tea and grasped the container by the sides instead of the handle. He let go and pulled back, startled.

"Watch out, the pot is hot!" I warned, too late. Billy hadn't noticed the waiter when he'd slipped a fresh pot on the table. I saw the pain in his eyes, and I couldn't tell if it was because of his oversight or my attack.

Billy dipped his three fingers into the half glass of water on the table and dried them on his napkin. "Is it wrong to have friends?" he asked, harkening back to my earlier comment.

The innocence of the question disarmed me. I was sure my father missed the point again.

"No. Of course not. Except when your friends become your lifeline, your reason to exist."

"Why'd you say that? Because I like to socialize? Hey, I enjoy myself. That a crime?"

"Only when it gets in the way of . . . ah, never mind. Let it go." I hesitated to bring up the issue of my graduation.

"Crap, never mind! Tell me! Except when it gets in the way of what?" Wide-eyed, Billy looked challenged. The owner, Chen, stared as he exited through the kitchen's swinging doors, balancing several steaming bags of outgoing orders.

"In the way of your family," I finally said.

Billy's eyes opened wider, and his mouth twisted. He became an engine with a flooded carburetor. "I never . . . I never . . . God, Nick! How the hell . . . I mean . . . good Lord . . . ."

"Dad, I'm sorry. Really, I'm sorry."

We remained silent. A lifetime passed. I watched Billy's ruddy hue disappear as his complexion returned to its normal pallor. When he spoke again, his voice had a scratchy texture.

"Nick, I never meant to put my friends ahead of my family, you and Claire."

"I know, Dad," I lied, "but you did. That's why I'm bitter. How do I make you understand? I missed my father. Not having one, I mean."

Billy appeared like a lost child as he tried to follow my words. The irony made me smile. "I needed a father as I was growing up," I continued. "I need a father now! I need you! Why the hell are you scared to be there?" My voice rose again.

"I ain't afraid. It's just . . . I mean . . . I don't know how to . . . 'least not the way you expect. I ain't no good at it, Nick."

When he said the words, they resonated like arrows hitting a target circle. They echoed the mantra Claire dogged me with every time she found the opportunity: "No matter how much you wish it, Billy will never be the father you want him to be, and if you can't accept him for who he is, you'll always be fatherless." Reading Billy's face, I understood his fear, his anguish.

"I'm sorry, Dad. I've been staring into a camera lens too long. My peripheral vision sucks."

Billy squeezed his right fist into his left palm like a pestle grinding a clove of garlic. His eyes studied the floor.

"Let's get the hell out of here, get some air." I covered the check with four twenties and saw my untouched ball of vanilla had melted into a pool of creamy liquid.

We exited the restaurant. The coolness of the night washed my face and cleared my eyes. The traffic along Queens Boulevard lighted our way to the parking lot. We walked without speaking until we reached Billy's car.

"Nick, I'm sorry too."

"Ah, forget it, Dad. We should have aired this out long ago. Guess I needed to look beyond my nose—tried harder to understand."

"Yeah, me too, Nick. You're right. I didn't do too great by you either, understanding how you felt and all that. Shoulda called you way before this. Listen to me. A lotta times horses stumble gettin' out of the gate. But if they don't lose heart, they can make it up down the stretch."

I put my arm across my father's shoulders. He turned to pull me into a bear hug, his body rocking with emotion.

When he let go, I stepped back and said, "Not too rough on you tonight, was I?"

A small grin broke at the corners of his mouth. "Naah, ya never laid a glove on me."

"Dad, you didn't finish what you were telling me at the table, something about pipes."

"Oh, yeah. Almost forgot. I had a physical last month, and I'm okay except they found this spot on my lungs. Not big, a small one. The doc wants me to quit smoking. As if I stopped, it would do any good. Besides, I quit and people wouldn't mistake me for Maurice Chevalier anymore," he said as he ducked his head through the opened car door. "I just need to take it easy," he told me.

I took hold of the top of the doorframe. "Hold on, for God's sake! Did you get a second opinion, let someone else examine you?"

"No. Why should I? Doc Stern's a fine physician. Been goin' to him most of my life."

"Dad, is he sure? I mean, this doesn't sound like something you should take lightly."

"Stop worryin'. The spot's a small one. The doc said he would keep a check on me."

"Well, how about cutting back on smoking? The way you chain smoke, you look more like Oscar Levant than Maurice Chevalier."

"Levant! He ain't even good lookin'," Billy said, turning on the ignition.

"Come on, Dad, I'm serious. Let me take you for another exam, just to make sure. There's a lung specialist in the building where I live."

"It ain't necessary, Nick, honest. Stern's keepin' an eye on me. Need a ride home?"

"No, I'll walk. My apartment is only a few blocks from here." I let go of the door and closed it. Billy waved, beeped the horn, then pulled away. "So long, Dad," I yelled. "Call you next week."

* * *

Early in the morning, three months later, Claire called with the news. I had arrived on the red-eye, exhausted and yet to unpack from a shooting assignment in Los Angeles. The conversation was brief and devastating.

"He has lung cancer. He's at Queens General Hospital."

My unsteady hand clutched the phone. "What's his condition? I mean, how far along?"

"The cancer has spread throughout. He's had it a lot longer than he let on. They brought him into the emergency room, falling down drunk. At first, they diagnosed it as cirrhosis of the liver but later discovered cancer in his lungs." Her controlled tone and calmness amazed me.

"Damn!" My mind flooded with feelings of desertion. "Why now? Just as I'm . . . I mean, it's only taken me thirty-five years to understand who the hell my father is."

"I'll pick you up after work, around six."

"No, don't bother, Claire. I'm going over there now. Call you later." After I hung up, I grabbed my coat and headed for the door. While I stood at the elevator, I visualized Billy in the hospital room, struggling to hang on through his network of tubes, the sounds of the respirator as his only companion. I worried he would close his eyes for the last time before he saw the understanding in mine.

The cab ride was deadly silent while the city came alive. I stared at the passing scenery as my mind raced.

What I visited through my internal viewfinder were horses flying down the soft, dirt surface of a racetrack stretch run, on hooves that never touched the ground. A lone colt, coming from behind, head down, ears back, passed the tightly bunched Thoroughbreds from the back of the pack, moving up on the outside in one mighty drive. As he took the lead and closed on the wire, I spotted his tail swishing playfully.

"Wait for me, Billy," I whispered. "Wait for me."

ACKNOWLEDGMENTS

I need to acknowledge three exceptional people who were responsible for my journey toward becoming a published author.

Ted Gottfried, author/instructor of the short story writing course he taught in 1990 at Baruch College in New York City. Ted imparted his understanding and knowledge of writing in this genre with careful and effective discourse. I benefitted greatly from his creative instruction, especially the wise counsel he offered at the term's end: "The real writing begins with the rewriting."

Ellen Feldman, author/leader of my critique group at Marymount College in New York City. A prolific fiction author, Ellen patiently guided our band of eager writers. She was thoughtful and honest with her critique; she once returned a submitted story with the comment, "You had me until the end; then you copped out." Years later, I expanded that story into my debut novel, *Tracking Terror*, and it became a contest award winner.

James Robeson, author/adjunct professor/leader of my critique group at Florida Gulf Coast University. Jim was always supportive in his criticism, and often employed humor to make his point. After months of critiquing my debut novel's progress in his class, Jim volunteered to edit the manuscript's first draft. Two weeks later, he apologized for taking so long, confessing, "I finished reading the first hundred pages and forgot I had an editing pencil in my hand." Magic words for any writer.

I'd like to thank Carole Greene not only for her usual thorough editing of these stories but for doing so with such a loving touch. Lastly, I'm also grateful to my publisher, BluewaterPress LLC, for believing that the short-story form is still alive and appreciated.

We hope you have enjoyed reading Howard Giordano's collections of short stories. If you have not had the chance to read his previous novels, may we suggest his novel of suspense, *Tracking Terror*. Another of his detective tales is *The Second Target* in which he introduces us to NYPD Detective Luke Rizzo. His third published novel with BluewaterPress LLC, *Crossing into Darkness*. *The Dark Side of the City* is another story involving Rizzo going after the Mafia.

Each of these books is an excellent read and available through BluewaterPress LLC, online at bluewaterpress.com, as well as other major online retailers.

www.ingramcontent.com/pod-product-compliance
Lightning Source LLC
Chambersburg PA
CBHW071526120726
47907CB00013B/1088